'Did y

Cal asked her

'Sorry?' She looked ~~~~~~ at him, pretending she hadn't heard, trying to play for time. What kind of question was that?

'Since we split up, have you ever had a moment when you missed me?'

She hesitated. The truth was she had missed him a lot. There had been days when she was desperate to talk to him, to ask him things. Like, why had this happened to them? Sometimes she'd missed him so badly she had lain in bed and ached for him. But she wouldn't tell him that.

'No, I don't think so.' She smiled airily at him. 'Sorry if that upsets your ego.'

Cal shrugged. 'I missed you,' he said softly.

Kathryn Ross was born in Zambia, where her parents happened to live at that time. Educated in Ireland and England, she now lives in a village near Blackpool, Lancashire. Kathryn is a professional beauty therapist, but writing is her first love. As a child she wrote adventure stories, and at thirteen was editor of her school magazine. Happily, ten writing years later, DESIGNED WITH LOVE was accepted by Mills & Boon®. A romantic Sagittarian, she loves travelling to exotic locations.

Recent titles by the same author:

THE ELEVENTH-MOVE GROOM
THE NIGHT OF THE WEDDING

HER DETERMINED HUSBAND

BY
KATHRYN ROSS

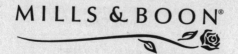

MILLS & BOON®

First published in Great Britain 2002
Harlequin Mills & Boon Limited,
Eton House, 18-24 Paradise Road, Richmond, Surrey TW9 1SR

© Kathryn Ross 2002

ISBN 0 263 82918 9

Set in Times Roman 10½ on 11¼ pt.
01-0302-52883

Printed and bound in Spain
by Litografia Rosés, S.A., Barcelona

CHAPTER ONE

IT WAS a fact of life that when you were running late for an appointment the traffic lights were always on red and you could never find a parking space. Then, when you did find a space, some arrogant so-and-so stole it! Kirsten glared angrily at the man in the snazzy convertible Mercedes who had just blatantly snuck into her coveted spot.

He turned and their eyes connected, and in that brief instant Kirsten felt numb with shock. It was her ex-husband, Cal McCormick.

As she drove on past and the eye contact was severed she immediately doubted her senses. No! It couldn't have been Cal, she tried to reassure herself. Cal wasn't in Hollywood; he wasn't even in America. He was still working in England, wasn't he?

She glanced in her rear-view mirror and saw the man climb out of the car. He was tall, with a good physique and dark hair, but she was at a distance now and it was too hard to say if it was Cal or not.

Forgetting the fact that she was rushing for an important luncheon appointment with her agent, Kirsten swung her old car once more around the block and went back for another look.

But the red car was locked up by the time she got back and there was no sign of the handsome man in the pale grey suit.

There were a million good-looking guys in LA and that man wasn't Cal, she told herself soothingly. A space became vacant further down the street and she drove into it with a shaky feeling of relief.

This wasn't the first time that she had thought she had glimpsed her ex-husband. It was two years since they had split up, but in the aftermath of their divorce she had imagined she had seen him on quite a few occasions...even whilst knowing full well that it couldn't be him because Cal was thousands of miles away on another shore with another woman.

But she was over all that now, and definitely over Cal McCormick. And this was no day for her to go to pieces, she told herself firmly. Things were going right for her now. She had auditioned for a leading role in an up-and-coming movie and out of hundreds of applicants had got the part. Her contract was signed and today she was to meet her co-star, Jack Boyd, and her agent, Gerry Woods, for lunch. This was the day that her fortunes changed, her bank balance reverted to the black and her ex-husband was wiped clear off her memory bank for ever.

She ran a smoothing hand over her long blonde hair, glanced at herself in her mirror to reassure herself that she looked her best, and then, taking a deep breath, stepped out onto the sidewalk.

From his vantage point of the best table in the exclusive restaurant, Cal watched Kirsten walk down the sidewalk towards him. She hadn't changed at all, he thought. Even viewed through a smoked-glass haze, she looked vibrantly fabulous. She was wearing a stylish white trouser suit that probably came from one of the designer boutiques in the town, and despite the fact that she was tall she wore incredibly high heels. Her thick blonde hair was loose and looked slightly windswept.

There were lots of good-looking blondes in Hollywood but Kirsten had something different about her. Maybe it was the fact that her hair was a natural colour of spun gold, maybe the fact that her figure was all her own as well, no silicone implants required for that slender, yet very shapely

body. Or maybe it was just the quiet intelligence that shone
from her eyes when she looked up. Whatever it was, she
still had a style that held his attention. He hurriedly returned
his gaze to the menu as she reached the doorway of the
restaurant, before she could catch him watching her.

He heard her accent, clearly discernible, from the front
reservation desk. Even though she had been living in the
States from the age of eleven, the low husky voice still
held the traces of her English accent. It brought back a
flood of memories.

Then she stood next to his table and he could smell the
scent of her perfume, warm, familiar, very evocative.

He stood up slowly and their eyes met for the second
time that morning.

'Hello, Kirsten,' he smiled.

'Cal…' His name sounded uncomfortable on her lips and
to say she looked shocked was putting it mildly. She
glanced over at the waiter. 'I think there has been some
mistake,' she said, sounding slightly breathless. 'I'm supposed to be meeting Gerry Woods; he made a table reservation for twelve-thirty?' She looked past the waiter and
around the restaurant, desperately searching for her agent.
It was hard to see who was in the room because the tables
were strategically placed for maximum privacy behind tall
plants and exotic flower arrangements. The fact that she
was in a blind panic didn't help either.

'This is Mr Woods's table.' The waiter pulled out a chair
for her and waited politely for her to seat herself.

She looked back at the starched white tablecloth with its
cut glasses and delicate orchid flower arrangement, then up
into Cal's eyes again.

'Gerry has been unavoidably detained, but he should be
here soon.' Cal sounded nonchalantly at ease, as if their
meeting was an everyday occurrence, when in fact they
hadn't seen each other for two years. Well, two years, one
month and three weeks to be exact, she thought, hating

herself for still carrying that useless information in her brain.

Cal sat back down and she was left with the decision of whether to sit with him, or to cause a scene and leave. Only because Gerry would be joining them soon, and she wanted to find out what was going on, she chose the former.

The waiter went through an elaborate routine of taking her napkin and shaking it out to place it over her knee, then he handed her a menu and distanced himself.

Her heart was thumping against her chest and she couldn't bring herself to look Cal directly in the eye again. This was terrible...really terrible. She felt overwhelmed with an emotion that she couldn't even begin to understand.

'So how are you, Kirsten?' Cal asked, reaching for the jug of water and pouring her a glass.

'I'm OK...how are you?' she managed politely after a moment. She forced herself to look at him again. He was thirty-eight, but if anything he looked even more handsome than when she had last seen him, his face still had that patrician, square-jawed, powerful attractiveness, and, although his dark, thick hair now had a few silver strands at the temples, they gave him a distinguished air.

She had almost forgotten how very blue his eyes were. They glimmered with amusement now, as if he knew how much effort it had taken her to sound courteous.

'I'm not much different from when you saw me last,' he replied easily. 'But thanks for asking.'

How right he was, Kirsten thought in bewilderment. She had always thought that if she saw him again it would be like meeting a stranger. But it didn't feel like that at all. Looking at him across this table felt disturbingly familiar; in fact it was as if someone had suddenly rolled back time and the last few years had disappeared.

It was a very odd sensation and Kirsten didn't like it at all. This was the man who had broken her heart, ripped it out and roasted it, in fact, and she didn't want to put time back. The road to recovery from Cal had been too long and painful to allow it to be smashed to pieces now.

'Well, now we've got the pleasantries over, would you like a drink?'

I need a drink, Kirsten thought, preferably a large one. 'What's going on, Cal?' she asked him, trying to gather her startled wits together. 'What are you doing here?'

He frowned. 'Didn't Gerry tell you?'

'Tell me what?' She had a horrible sensation in the pit of her stomach as if she was on a fairground ride, being hauled up a steep incline with the uncertain knowledge of how huge the drop was on the other side.

'That we are going to be working together.'

'Sorry?' She wondered if she had misheard him.

'I've been offered the lead part in this new film you are signed up for.'

He watched the incredulity in her eyes. 'Yes, it's a bit ironic, isn't it?' he agreed. 'We'll be husband and wife once more…just on the silver screen this time, of course.'

'This is some kind of joke, right?' Her voice was very unsteady. 'Gerry told me that this movie is being made by some company called Sugar Productions and Jack Boyd has been given the lead part.'

Cal shook his head. 'The name of the production company is right. But I've got the lead part, not Jack.'

The fairground ride tipped over the edge and she was given a dizzying, terrifying glimpse down into an interminable abyss. Her finances were shaky, and she needed this job…but she couldn't work closely with her ex-husband, especially for the length of time it took to make a movie! It was more than mere flesh and blood could stand.

Her mobile phone rang suddenly and unexpectedly, releasing Kirsten from her frozen state of immobility. She reached for her handbag, knocking over her glass of water in her haste.

A waiter materialised by her elbow to wipe up the flood

as she pushed her chair back. 'Sorry…' She tried to smile apologetically at him as she pushed herself even further away and looked at her phone. The name 'Gerry' was flashing in green letters.

She pressed the connect button. 'Hi, Gerry, where are you?' Hidden behind the polite words were the more desperate ones, like, Where the hell are you? Come and bail me out of this mess you've got me into.

'Stuck in traffic; Kirsten, I'm real sorry about this.'

Not as sorry as he was going to be, she thought grimly as she met Cal's calm gaze across the table.

'You didn't tell me about the change of co-star.' She lowered her tone even more, but there was a dangerous edge to it.

'That's because I didn't know until a few hours ago.'

Why didn't she believe him? Kirsten wondered suddenly.

'Great news, isn't it?' Gerry continued blithely. 'It's a real coup for the studio. They can't believe their luck…I mean, Cal is one of the biggest names in Hollywood, a fantastic actor, a real heart throb, it will boost the film's ratings no end—'

Kirsten allowed him to prattle on and meanwhile there was this cold, churning sensation in the pit of her stomach. When her agent paused for breath she said very quickly, very coolly, 'I'm sorry, Gerry, but this isn't going to work.'

'Why not?' Gerry sounded genuinely perplexed.

'Because he's my ex-husband,' she said succinctly, as if she was talking to someone who was quite mad.

She glanced across at Cal and saw the glint of mockery in his blue eyes now. But she was past caring what he thought; she just wanted out of this.

'You're not serious, Kirsten!' Gerry laughed. 'If everyone in Hollywood decided they couldn't work together because they'd once had a relationship, nobody would be making any films!'

'I don't care.' Her voice rose slightly and with difficulty

she lowered it and forced herself to remain calm. 'I don't care what everyone else does—'

'You've already signed the contract.' Gerry started to sound impatient.

'I signed, thinking I was acting alongside Jack—'

'That doesn't make a difference to the studio. If you renege on your contract they'll sue us, Kirsten…it will cost fortunes. You're due to start filming next week.'

Kirsten could hear a tremor of nerves underneath Gerry's firm tone, but it was nothing compared to what was going on inside Kirsten. She had thought all her money worries were over when she signed this film contract. Now she felt like an animal caught in a trap, waiting for certain death.

'Look, you go ahead and have lunch without me, talk things over with Cal. He's a real nice guy and a professional. I'm sure you two can come to a good agreement about working alongside each other. I'll ring you later.'

The phone went dead.

'Problems?' Cal asked innocently from the other side of the table.

Her eyes narrowed on him. She knew full well that he must have heard everything…and the bits he hadn't heard he was probably able to fill in for himself.

'Gerry is stuck in traffic. He says for us to go ahead and eat without him.' She forced herself to remain civil, her mind rushing ahead, working on the problem. If she couldn't get out of the film, maybe she could appeal to the better side of her ex's nature and get him to stand down. After all, as Gerry had said, Cal was a big name in Hollywood; he could work anywhere. And possibly the idea of working with her wasn't too pleasing to him either.

She moved closer to the table. 'I'll just have a mineral water, please?' she asked the waiter with a smile as he finished tidying up the mess she had made. 'And I'll try not to knock it over this time. Sorry about that.'

At least to outward appearances she sounded as if she

had pulled herself together again, Kirsten thought. She couldn't let Cal know how traumatised she felt just sitting opposite him. He'd find that very amusing.

She stalled for time, putting her phone away in her bag. 'So, when did you realise you were going to have to work alongside me on this film?' she asked him, trying to sound casual.

'I'd heard something vaguely, but only knew for definite this morning.'

'I see.' She glanced across at him. 'And are you as delighted about the prospect as I am?' There was an edge of sarcasm in her tone.

'I don't know,' Cal retorted imperturbably. 'How delighted are you?'

Her smile became overstretched. He knew damn well that she was fizzing. Was he deliberately trying to wind her up?

'I didn't even know you were back State-side.' She tried a roundabout approach. Playing for time.

'Yes, I got back about a month ago. I'm renting a house in Beverly Hills.'

'Nice.' Kirsten thought about the small apartment that she was sharing with her flatmate Chloe. It had two small bedrooms and a living room and a kitchen hardly big enough for three people to be in at the same time.

Cal seemed to have gone from strength to strength since they had divorced, whilst her career had been severely handicapped by her last agent. Robin Chandler had signed her up soon after she had split up with Cal. At the time she had been a successful singer with a string of hits in the American charts. Chandler had promised promotion and world tours, but what she'd got was an agent who took all her money and tied her up in legal jargon that made it impossible for her to continue her singing career for a full two years without lining his pockets even further.

All her money, even the generous divorce settlement Cal

had insisted on making to her, had disappeared into the black hole that had been her time with Robin Chandler. She had sought legal advice, but in the end she had been in so much debt that she had decided to cut her losses and wait until the time limit on her contract with Chandler expired. Her career as a recording artist on hold, she had desperately needed to find other work, so she had switched agents and followed Gerry's advice into the world of acting.

She was still surprised by her success in this field. Even though her talent as a musician had led her to stage school as a child, she had never envisaged herself becoming an actress.

Up until now she had only had supporting roles but each had added to her reputation as a fine actress. And now she had been offered the chance to move into the movies, and her first leading part, which promised more lucrative rewards and an opportunity to finally turn the corner from financial ruin towards more secure times.

'How are your parents?' Cal interrupted her thoughts.

She returned her attention to him, meeting his gaze steadily across the table, and the hope of more tranquil times ahead seemed uncertain again. Her mum and dad had loved Cal; he had charmed them almost as easily as he had charmed her. 'They're fine,' she said tightly, and then found herself relenting slightly. 'Well, actually Dad hasn't been very well.'

'What's the matter with him?'

Kirsten stared across the table at him; he was a good actor, she thought, because he honestly looked as if he gave a damn. She shrugged, not about to go into details with him. 'I don't know; they're running tests.' Thinking about her dad put things in perspective for a moment. He was going into hospital for the day on Wednesday and she kept telling herself not to worry, that whatever was wrong would be fixed, but every now and then she couldn't help her mind running anxiously over worst-case scenarios.

Cal heard the apprehension in her tone, saw the shadows in her green eyes, and for a moment he was strongly tempted to reach across the table and take her hand. But that would be a very big mistake, he told himself grimly.

'Are they still living out near San Francisco?' he asked instead.

'Yes…and Dad's still got his fishing boat.' For the briefest second a smile lit her face, transforming it into radiant loveliness. He was reminded vividly of the first weekend she had taken him to meet her folks, how they'd taken the boat out on a clear summer afternoon.

Then as she met his gaze again it was as if the clouds settled over the green of the sea and her smile vanished.

'Give them both my best wishes next time you're speaking to them,' Cal said.

She shrugged. She didn't like to mention Cal's name to her mum and dad, but she wouldn't give him the pleasure of telling him that, of letting him know how much he'd hurt them as well.

The waiter put a small bottle of water down next to her. In the space of silence she forced herself to turn her attention to the present.

'So what are we going to do about this film?' she asked briskly.

'We're going to act in it, I presume.'

'Don't be facetious, Cal, it doesn't help,' she snapped. 'And anyway,' she added in a cooler, quieter voice, 'I was hoping that I was going to act in the film and you were going to do the decent, gentlemanly thing and bow out.'

'Why would I do that?' He looked genuinely perplexed. 'I wouldn't dream of backing out. I've given my word—'

'For all that's worth,' she couldn't resist grating sarcastically and then immediately regretted the slip. She wasn't going to get anywhere making remarks like that. 'Anyway,' she continued hurriedly, thinking maybe it would just be best to be straight with him, 'as you probably gathered from my telephone call just now, I don't want to work alongside you, Cal, it's as simple as that.'

'Then maybe you should be the one to back out,' he said. 'Because I'm not going anywhere. I've signed to do this film and I'm looking forward to it.'

He'd already signed the contract! Her heart lurched with fear. 'Are you doing this to annoy me?' she hissed, her control breaking, her eyes narrowing. 'This film is my first big break in ages and you're deliberately trying to sabotage it.'

'Don't be ridiculous. You should be thanking me, not asking me to leave. My name will make all the difference to the sales of the film. I've probably rescued it from life as a B-movie.'

'You're as modest as ever,' she cut across him scathingly.

He smiled at her. 'But you know what I'm saying is true. Look on the bright side—you might be nominated for an award, working alongside me.'

'A purple heart for bravery, you mean? And you could probably get a gold medal in annoying me,' she reflected pensively.

His lips twisted in a rueful grin. 'Nothing personal,' he told her with a glint of devilment in his blue gaze, and for the briefest second she saw him through the American public's eyes.

It was no wonder they queued up for hours at the cinema to see him; he had a magnetic quality about him, an air of dangerous excitement as well as those undeniably fabulous looks. She had often wondered if he was so successful because he was a complete enigma, you couldn't really pigeon-hole him anywhere. Although he was American through and through, he had been educated in Oxford, England, and he had worked for an English newspaper before returning home and getting a job as a sports correspondent. Writing fiction in his spare time, he had fallen into a lead role in Hollywood because of a script that he had written for them.

She had fallen for the whole dangerous package before he had made it into the big time. So in a way she had stolen a march on those fans; she knew exactly how they felt when they sat watching him in awe in the darkened cinema. She had been taken in as well.

In fact, the moment Kirsten had met Cal McCormick a kind of madness had descended upon her. Within a whirlwind period of four months they were married and then eleven months later filing for divorce.

Kirsten likened it to an illness, and afterwards referred to that period of her life as the time when she had 'Calinitus'. He'd clouded her judgement, crept insidiously into her heart and had taken her over completely.

When he smiled with that teasing grin, as he did now, and a woman felt the full power of his looks, he could get away with anything. But not with her, she reminded herself; she had his measure. And if telling her that the movie would only do well because he was in it wasn't a personal attack on her acting skills, she didn't know what was, she thought furiously.

She picked up the menu, playing for time, to gather her thoughts sensibly. She wasn't going to get anywhere losing her temper with him; she knew that from past experience.

'How come you're not concentrating on your singing career these days?' Cal asked her suddenly. 'You haven't made a record for ages.'

Kirsten was surprised by the change of subject and wary of answering because she didn't want to tell him what a dreadful mistake she had made with her last agent. 'I just decided I needed a change, that's all,' she murmured evasively.

'I never thought you would go into acting.'

'Neither did I.' She smiled for a moment. 'But I changed my manager and Gerry suggested I audition for a role on Broadway. It was just a small cameo part, but I did well to get it. It was a tremendous challenge.'

At the time she hadn't been at all sure about the move. She remembered flying to New York for the audition, wondering if she was wasting money that she could ill afford on plane tickets and hotels, but out of hundreds of hopefuls she had been selected.

That role had launched her new career in style. The show had been a major success and the critics had loved her. Although it had only been scheduled to run for four months, they had extended it to six. And, on her return to LA, it had opened doors for her into the acting world.

'So the only reason you went into acting was because you wanted a challenge?'

Why was he continuing to question her? Kirsten wondered angrily. It was none of his business why she had turned away from her career as a recording artist. 'Yes, something like that,' she murmured. She was damned if she was going to tell him that because of her dodgy agent she'd had no choice but to go into acting.

The waiter interrupted them. He put an ice bucket and a bottle of champagne next to the table and placed two long-stemmed glasses between them.

'What's the champagne for?' Kirsten eyed it apprehensively, as if it were a bomb waiting to go off.

'I've no idea.' Cal shrugged. 'Rest assured I didn't order it.'

'With the compliments of Mr Gerry Woods,' the waiter informed them both with a polite smile. 'Would you like me to pour it now, sir?' he asked into the silence.

'No, thanks, I'll pour it,' Cal said.

As the waiter hovered, waiting for them to order their food, Kirsten hurriedly glanced down at the menu and ordered the first thing she saw.

Why was her agent sending them champagne? she wondered as they were left alone again. This was getting out of hand.

'Look, Cal, I'm asking you nicely. Please tell the studio you won't be available for this movie after all.' She hoped there was no hint in her tone of the desperation she was suddenly feeling. She needed this part. It would be the first really decent money she had earned in ages, and she had worked very hard to get here. Stood in long queues and auditioned several times. By contrast Cal could walk into a part anywhere.

'I'm sorry, Kirsten, but I can't do that,' he replied calmly. 'I've told you, I've already signed the contract.'

She watched as he poured sparkling champagne into the flutes and felt helpless. She hated the feeling of not being in control; it made her angry. It brought back memories of her relationship with Cal.

'Your agent is obviously very happy with the situation…so happy he's sent champagne. He must know how this is going to do you nothing but favours. Trust me on this.'

'I'd rather trust a barracuda not to bite,' she retorted. 'And for your information I don't need any favours from you,' she added quickly. 'I'm doing very well on my own.'

Cal looked at her across the table. 'I'm sure you are.' The quiet way he said those words unnerved her slightly.

Made her wonder if he knew about Robin Chandler and the backlog of bills she was still working her way through.

She looked away. He couldn't know about that. She had been very careful to tell no one, not even her parents…especially her parents; they would have worried themselves sick. The only people she had confided in were her flatmate, Chloe, and Jason. And they were her best friends, the souls of discretion.

'And now you are going to do even better,' he added firmly. 'Look, Kirsten, this is business, pure and simple.

There is nothing personal between us any longer. I don't see why we should have any problem acting opposite each other. It's just work.' He shrugged. 'I can't for the life of me understand where you are coming from with this panic-stricken "please leave" routine.'

'I'm not panic-stricken.' She sat straighter in her chair.

'So what's the problem?'

She stared at him and tried to think of a suitable, sensible reply. How was it that Cal always made her feel as if she was the one in the wrong, that she was the unreasonable one? He had a real knack for wrong-footing her.

'I've told you what the problem is.' She tried to remain firm. 'Do I have to spell it out in black and white? I don't want you around.'

'Do you know what I think?' He leaned forward across the table and instinctively she leaned back warily.

'I think you are frightened of me.'

'Oh, please! Why the hell should I be frightened of you?' she scoffed.

'I don't know, maybe my manly presence upsets you.'

She stared at him and saw the twinkle of amusement in his blue eyes. 'You always did have a warped sense of humour,' she said tautly. 'And for your information your manly presence doesn't cause me a second thought.'

'That's not what you used to say.' His voice was deep and husky and disturbingly sexy. It disturbed a cauldron of emotion that Kirsten very definitely didn't want stirring.

Kirsten had never been so glad to see a waiter approach in all her life. She looked down at the plate of food that he put before her and tried not to think about Cal's words. But he was right, of course; there had been a time when he had only to look at her to turn her on.

'Gerry seems a decent kind of guy,' Cal continued as he liberally sprinkled his steak with salt.

'He's OK.'

'Better than that other agent you went to after we split up. What was his name…Chandler?'

Kirsten felt her blood pressure rising. 'Chandler was all right,' she lied.

'Really? I heard that a few people in town got their fingers badly burnt by him, and that you did well to get out when you did.'

Trouble was she hadn't got out soon enough, Kirsten thought as she pushed her food around the plate.

When she said nothing he shrugged. 'But I could have heard wrong. I've been working out of the country for two years, so what would I know.'

'Yes, what would you know?' Her voice grated roughly. She hoped that Cal would never find out what an idiot she had been to trust Chandler. She felt foolish enough.

'I still think you should have gone to that guy who handled Maeve.'

Hasn't everyone handled Maeve? Kirsten wanted to ask derisively, but bit down on her lip.

'Maeve is going from strength to strength now.'

The last thing Kirsten wanted to hear was how well Maeve was doing. It inflamed her senses to even think about that woman. 'Yes, well, Maeve married a powerful director,' Kirsten couldn't help remarking tersely. 'It boils down to the same old adage, doesn't it…it's not what you know but who you know that counts? Personally I'd rather stand on my own two feet any day than have to marry for my career.'

'Well, maybe you've never been that hungry,' Cal said quietly.

'And Maeve has?' Kirsten's tone was brittle.

'I was talking about being hungry for success…but, seeing as you are asking, yes, Maeve has had tough times.'

A shaft of pain hit through Kirsten. He was still sticking up for Maeve, still in love with her after all this time. She'd have thought that he might have grown tired of waiting in the sidelines for that woman to get a divorce. But it seemed not; the situation must suit them both.

Kirsten had always known that there were people who preferred the thrill of the chase, the illicit affair rather than commitment, but it had come as something of a shock to find that she was married to one of those people. Cal had fooled her totally.

Originally she had felt sorry for Maeve's husband, Brian; he was a lot older than she was. But she had heard a whisper since that Brian had indulged in his share of affairs himself. Well, good luck to them all, Kirsten thought angrily. It certainly didn't suit her tastes. She was glad she had walked away from it.

'Tell me, what part did Maeve play in this film you've just finished making in England? Was she the serving wench, or the gold-digger?'

'You haven't lost your sense of humour anyway.' He reached across and refilled her glass.

'Why are you still so angry with me, Kirsten?' he asked suddenly, with that quiet, disarming directness that always unnerved her. 'You divorced me, if you remember, not the other way around.'

Was he serious? She wanted to scream at him in that second. The divorce had been a formality. OK, in a rare flash of gentlemanly behaviour he'd allowed her to file for it. But what choice had she had?

She stared at him, her green eyes shimmering with a kind of mutant dislike. What did he expect? she wondered. After the way he had treated her, what the hell did he expect?

She reached for her champagne. 'I'm not angry,' she said coldly. 'That would mean I gave a damn.'

The champagne left a bitter taste in her mouth, which was strange; champagne had never done that before.

'You know, Kirsten we were both under a lot of strain two years ago. I don't think either of us was thinking very clearly.'

The gentleness of his tone made her stomach twist in knots.

'No couple should ever have to go through what we went through.'

She looked down at her hands and tried to close her ears and her mind to the soft words. If he mentioned the unmentionable she would leave, she told herself. She'd just get up and walk out.

'When I got to England I tried to ring you several times.' He changed tack. 'But you never took my calls.'

'What was the point?' She looked up at him, relieved that he wasn't going to delve into the darker area of their break-up. 'The day you left our marriage was over.'

She saw the flash of annoyance in his eyes and found herself feeling pleased. Pleased that she could inflict just a tiny proportion of the hurt she had felt back on him. 'Anyway, I don't want to have this conversation,' she told him firmly. 'I don't even want to be here.'

'So I gathered.' His tone was dry. 'But we've got a lot of filming…a lot of work to get through together. I reckon we could do with calling a truce for a while, don't you?'

She hesitated.

'We can't change the past. We can only go forward and learn from it.'

He sounded so sensible, so mature. She knew he was right, but she couldn't forgive and forget.

'What do you say?' he asked. 'Shall we put our personal differences aside and work smoothly together?'

What choice did she have? she asked herself dismally. She couldn't get out of working on the film and he obviously wasn't going to do the decent thing and walk away from his part in it. So the only thing she could do was to try and at least tolerate his presence; otherwise the next few months were going to be hell. She shrugged. 'I don't want to work with you, but I've already signed the contract.'

'So that's a yes, then?' he asked sardonically.

'It's an I'll try,' she said huskily, the words sticking in her throat.

'Good.' He smiled. 'I'll look forward to working with you, Kirsten. I've read the reviews about your performance on Broadway. They say you've got talent.'

'You don't need to try to flatter me, Cal,' she murmured. 'A healthy respect between us will suffice.'

He raised his champagne glass. 'I'll drink to that.'

She didn't join him in the toast.

'Would you like a coffee?' he asked as she straightened her cutlery on the plate of untouched food.

'No. I'd like to go,' she said.

He didn't argue.

She watched as he summoned a waiter to ask for the bill.

He was probably happy now, thinking that everything was smoothed out between them, thinking that Cal the charmer was victorious again and that they could sweep the past tidily away out of sight. Work could go ahead unimpeded, and that was all Cal really cared about, she thought angrily.

'So, I'll see you next week on set,' he said as she got to her feet.

'Yes, see you next week.' She kept her voice light with difficulty. She could be as businesslike as him, she told herself confidently. Cal the charmer would never triumph over her again.

CHAPTER TWO

'YOU know *I've* always loved you.'

Kirsten's voice sounded stiff and unnatural even to her own ears. She glanced down at the script on the kitchen table, and read the line again, but it didn't sound any better; in fact, it sounded worse.

'Are you still working on that one line?' Her flatmate Chloe came in and grinned at her with genuine amusement.

'This is no laughing matter, Chloe.' Kirsten glanced at the kitchen clock. 'I've got to leave for the studio in five minutes and I'm still no closer to getting a handle on this part.'

'You'll be OK once you get on set. It's just first-day nerves.'

'Do you think?' Kirsten wanted to believe that, but honestly she had never felt as nervous as this before.

'I know so,' Chloe smiled. 'But I think you'd better have a look at this before you leave.' She slipped a glossy magazine down on top of Kirsten's script.

'Are you still buying these gossip rags...?' Kirsten's voice trailed off as she looked down and saw a picture of herself and Cal leaving Charlie's restaurant after their lunch together last week.

The headline read, *Is Hollywood heartthrob Cal McCormick getting back together again with his ex-wife?*

Kirsten tore her eyes away from the article without reading it. 'Who the hell took that photograph?' she asked. 'I didn't see any reporters outside that restaurant.'

'Well, you know what they're like, they were probably hiding up a tree.' Chloe grinned. 'Do you want me to read it to you while you get ready?'

'No, I do not.' Kirsten pushed it away. 'I'm ready to go anyway. Hell, I hope my mother hasn't read that!'

'Kirsten, half of Hollywood has probably read it. That's why I thought I'd better show it to you now before you leave. In case anybody says anything.'

'Thanks, I think.' Kirsten snatched up her script and her car keys. 'On that happy note, I had better go,' she said, sliding dark sunglasses down over her face.

It was only a fifteen-minute drive to the studios. Kirsten flashed her pass to the man on the gate and drove onto the lot with a feeling of doom firmly settled in her stomach. Noticing that the car in the reserved space next to hers had Cal's name on it didn't help. He'd probably been here since six this morning, and knew his lines backwards and inside out.

After the fierce heat of the Californian sun it was dark and cool inside the studios. Kirsten made her way to her dressing room and found that the girls from Wardrobe and Hairdressing were already in there.

'Morning, everyone.' She tried to smile cheerfully, as if she hadn't a care in the world, then she noticed the blue negligee hanging alone on the rails. 'What's that?' she asked suspiciously.

'That's your costume.'

'I thought we were doing an outdoor scene today?'

'Change of plan.' Mel, the hairdresser, smiled. 'They're shooting a bedroom scene instead.'

Kirsten tried to keep her smile firmly in place but she could feel it slipping. This was all she needed on her first morning.

Over an hour later, when Kirsten was left alone in her dressing room, she stared at her reflection in the mirror and tried to persuade herself that a bedroom scene wasn't such a big deal.

Luckily *The Love Child* was a light-hearted romantic comedy and the bedroom scenes weren't too steamy. There was no full nudity, just a lot of provocative kissing and canoodling between her and Cal, who played the part of Jonathan, her partner.

'But you're just acting a part,' Kirsten told her reflection sternly. 'You're Helen, not Kirsten, you don't even look like Kirsten any more.'

It was true that after her session in Hair and Make-up she did look different. Her hair was loose and wilder than usual; it tumbled in a riot of glossy waves over her shoulders. She was wearing a lot of make-up that had been skilfully applied to give her a natural, fresh-faced look, covering the fact that she hadn't slept well last night. And the sexily provocative full-length blue negligee was something that Kirsten would never have chosen to wear in a million years; it was far too revealing.

'You can do this,' she told herself again. The words rang hollowly inside her.

What on earth was the matter with her? she wondered. She had done a bedroom scene in a TV drama last year and hadn't thought twice about it. But then she had been acting alongside Jason Giles and Jason was a good friend. He'd made her laugh on set and it had all been very relaxed.

She thought about Jason fondly for a moment. They'd first met at a party in Hollywood when she and Cal had still been together. Then by coincidence they had been working on the same show on Broadway in New York and the same TV drama last year. His friendship had helped her through some difficult times in her life. She still saw him regularly; in fact, they were going to a première together at the weekend.

What she needed to do was think about this bedroom scene in the same relaxed way as the one with Jason last year. Why was she finding it so difficult to get into her character?

A picture of Cal's teasing grin and blue eyes rose in her mind and she felt suddenly sick with nerves again.

Maybe some meditation would help, she thought desperately. Chloe swore by meditation, and she had shown Kirsten how to use it as a method of unwinding.

She glanced at her watch. She had ten minutes before she needed to be on set. Quickly she sat down on the floor and crossed her legs in the lotus position, then, putting her thumb and forefinger together, she closed her eyes and tried to focus her mind and slow her breathing.

That was how Cal found her ten minutes later, sitting in the cramped, confined space between the dressing table and the clothes rails, humming softly under her breath. It was obvious she hadn't heard him enter the room because she didn't move or open her eyes.

He took the opportunity to watch her unobserved for a few seconds. She looked very young, probably about twenty-two or -three, yet he knew for a fact that she was thirty-one. She also looked incredibly sexy in the blue negligee. It dipped very provocatively over the full, creamy curve of her breasts and showed the slender lines of her body to perfection.

For a moment he found himself remembering when Kirsten had been his wife. Remembering her warmth and her passion and the hot nights when they had lain entwined in each other's arms, desire and need raging out of control.

He moved further into the room and her eyes flicked wide open in shocked surprise. 'What are you doing in here?' she demanded angrily. 'How dare you come in without knocking?'

'I did knock and I thought I heard you say come in.'

'Well, I didn't!' Her eyes moved over him. He was wearing a dark suit that sat well on his broad shoulders and he looked disturbingly handsome, too handsome for any woman's peace of mind.

But, as her grandma in Yorkshire would have said, handsome is as handsome does…or something along those lines.

She tried to keep that fact in mind as she met his amused gaze.

'If you don't mind my asking, what the heck are you doing down there on the floor?' he drawled laconically.

'I was meditating. Not that it's any of your business.'

'I see.' His lips twitched in amusement. 'Is it some new acting technique?'

'It's to help me relax,' she said tightly. 'What do you want, Cal? Or have you just come in here to insult me?' She ignored his helping hand as she got to her feet.

'I'd never insult you, Kirsten,' he said softly, his eye drifting down over the curves of her figure.

Conscious suddenly of her scanty attire, she reached for the silk dressing gown that matched her nightdress and threw it on.

'I just wanted to ask if you're OK with this sex scene we're going to do this morning?'

'Sex scene?' She gathered the robe around herself like a shield, and at the same time she felt her throat tighten in alarm. 'It isn't a sex scene, Cal.'

'We are about to get into bed together and your body is going to be pressed tightly against mine as we kiss…amongst other things.' His voice lowered huskily, his eyes sparked with humour. 'So what would you like me to call it?'

She tried not to blush or look in the slightest bit uncomfortable. 'What do you mean…amongst what other things?' she asked and despite her best efforts she knew she sounded rattled. 'It's a bedroom scene, Cal; sorry to disappoint you, but there's no sex in the film at all.'

'Isn't there?' He frowned. 'That's disappointing. And it's not what our esteemed director Theodore Tradaski was telling me a few moments ago.'

Kirsten tried to remain calm. He was just winding her up. 'It's one kiss, Cal, and I shall have to grit my teeth in order to bear even that much.'

To Kirsten's consternation, Cal didn't seem to be put out by her words. 'Good! I like a challenge to my acting skills. We'll see how long you manage to resist my charms, then, shall we?'

'What does that mean?' Her eyes narrowed warily.

'I think you know what it means,' he murmured. 'You pretend to grit your teeth and hate me and I'll do what I was always good at and turn you on.'

'You are insufferable sometimes, do you know that?' she told him heatedly, trying not to look as mortified by his crass remarks as she felt.

'Only sometimes?' he asked in mock disappointment.

Someone knocked on the door behind him. 'A bouquet of flowers has arrived for you, Kirsten,' a voice called cheerfully.

Cal turned and stepped out of the door. One of the stage-hands was outside; she was practically hidden behind an enormous bouquet of red roses.

'Oh, Mr McCormick, I didn't realise you were in here,' she gushed, her voice filled with a kind of reverence that made Kirsten feel nauseous.

'It's OK, I was just leaving.' Cal's eyes flicked over the bouquet. 'Who are the flowers from?' he asked casually.

Much to Kirsten's consternation, the woman opened the card that accompanied the flowers. 'They're from Jason Giles.' she told him eagerly. 'The message reads…'

Kirsten started to move to take the flowers away from her but she wasn't quick enough.

'…"Break a leg, Kirsty, I know you'll be terrific. I look forward to our date on Saturday at the première."'' The woman smiled up at Cal. 'Oh, and he's put some little kisses on the bottom.'

'Excuse me!' Kirsten whipped the bouquet from the stunned woman's hands. 'That's a private card!'

'Oh, sorry!' The woman pulled a face and then caught

Cal's eye and blushed and grinned at him in a conspiring way.

As the woman bustled back down the corridor—probably to tell the whole of the set what was written on her flowers, Kirsten thought in annoyance—Cal lingered in the doorway. 'Little kisses on the bottom?' he drawled mockingly.

'That card was none of your business—'

'I can't believe that Jason Giles is still hanging hopefully around you,' Cal continued with a frown. 'Why don't you put him out of his misery and get rid of him?'

'Because I don't want to get rid of him,' she told him tersely. 'Jason and I are very close.'

'Really?' He gave her a very disdainful look.

'Yes…really.' She supposed she was exaggerating. Jason was just a friend. But she did value his friendship; it had helped keep her together after her divorce.

'So how long has he been giving you these little kisses on the bottom, then?' Cal drawled wryly. 'Did it start on Broadway or as soon as I vacated the marital home?'

'Don't judge everyone by your own low standards,' she told him heatedly.

'Oh, come on, Kirsten! From what I've heard, the sheets had barely cooled on our bed before he was around knocking on your door.'

'Jason came around to offer his moral support. He's a wonderful person and I resent the distasteful implications in that statement.'

'You're certainly very protective of him. You must have it bad.'

'Go to hell, Cal.' She slammed the door shut.

It was only when the door closed that it suddenly dawned on Kirsten that Cal was fully dressed in his suit. They were supposed to be shooting a bedroom scene in a few minutes, so how come she was the only one dressed for bed? She glanced again at her watch. He should at least be wandering around in a dressing gown by now.

Maybe he was such a big star now that he didn't care if he was late on set? Maybe he intended to keep them all waiting? She frowned; that didn't sound like the Cal she remembered. Back in the days when they had been married, he had always had a thing about being punctual, and used to hate it if she was even a couple of minutes late for anything. Of course, he hadn't been such a phenomenally big star back then—moderately successful…but nothing more. Maybe all this mega-stardom had gone to his head.

Well, if he thought she was going to stand around kicking her heels in this scanty costume he had another thought coming. Kirsten took her time and found a vase and water for her flowers, then sat for a while in the warmth of her dressing room.

She found herself thinking about Cal's taunting gibe. 'You pretend to grit your teeth and hate me and I'll do what I was always good at and turn you on.'

In his dreams, she told herself staunchly. Then frowned. Well, maybe once upon a time he had very definitely been able to turn her on, she had to admit that if only to herself, but those days were long gone. When his lips touched hers now she would hate it.

She looked at her watch again and apprehensively she got to her feet. She supposed she had better not push her luck too far. She didn't want the director tearing her off a strip on the first day of filming. Theodore was supposed to be a brilliant director, but he had an unfortunate reputation for losing his temper.

When she appeared on set she half expected them all to be waiting for her, but there was some kind of altercation going on at the other side of the studio between the electricians and Theodore and no one seemed to notice her amidst the chaos.

There were teams of people still moving furniture around on the set. Picking her way carefully across electric cables, she stood in the shadows for a moment and watched. It looked as if they weren't going to start filming yet for at least another hour.

A spotlight was thrown on, and a huge double bed with a gothic wrought-iron headboard was illuminated in its bright glare.

'The scene of the battlefield.' Cal's sardonic tone resounded suddenly in her ear, making her gaze swing away from the double bed in shock.

'Crikey Cal! Don't creep up on me like that,' she said crossly. 'You nearly made me jump out of my skin.'

'Your nerves must be bad. What were you thinking about?' He smiled. 'Don't tell me you were daydreaming about our romantic scene together? It will be just like the old days.'

'A horror story, you mean?' she muttered. 'Why aren't you ready to get into bed with me?' she asked with a frown as she noticed he was still dressed in his suit.

'Kirsty, I'm always ready to get into bed with you,' he drawled sardonically.

'You know what I mean, Cal.' She shot him a warning look. 'I'm here in costume, ready to shoot the scene; you look as if you're still wearing your own clothes.'

'No...the suit is courtesy of Wardrobe. This is not something I'd have chosen to wear.'

It looked suspiciously like one of his suits to her. 'But shouldn't you be...in a state of undress?'

Cal's lips twitched. 'I don't think Theo is going to shoot the scene as it was first written.'

'What's he going to do?' Kirsten asked in consternation as she remembered his gibes earlier about a sex scene.

Cal shrugged. 'I don't know. He's the director.'

The possibility of a more intimate love scene being shot made her shiver violently. 'But I've learnt all my lines; he can't change things at this late time—'

'Theodore is running the show, Kirsten, he can do pretty much anything he likes.' Cal reached and straightened her dressing gown over her shoulder, bringing her attention to the fact that it had slipped.

The gentle touch of his hand against her bare arm made her shiver again. Suddenly she was very aware of how close he was standing to her, the gleam in his eye as he looked down at her. She started to feel breathless as she looked up at him. Nervously she moistened her lips as she felt his gaze linger on their softness. Her heart was pumping heavily against her chest.

She found herself remembering the way he used to kiss her, the heat of his lips and his hands against her body. She couldn't get into bed and pretend to make love with him, she just couldn't!

'You're not really nervous, are you, Kirsten?' he asked her suddenly, his voice gentle.

'No, of course not. Why would I be nervous?' Her voice was higher than it should have been. Hell, this was making a mockery of all her stern words about how strong she was, how his kiss wouldn't have any effect on her. He only had to brush his hand against her arm and she was in panic mode.

'Shall we run through our lines while we're waiting?' he asked her suddenly.

'No!' Kirsten forced herself to move back from him. 'What's the point if Theo is changing the script already?'

'Maybe you're right.' Cal glanced past her. 'Here's the man himself, so we're about to find out.'

Theodore was a tall man of about fifty. He had wiry dark hair and eyes that were so dark and intense they could drill holes in you with just a glance. Kirsten didn't really know him; she had only met him a couple of times. But she had heard about his fearsome reputation for flying into rages.

He looked as if he was living up to his reputation today; his face was red with anger and he was muttering something under his breath.

'Theo, what's the problem?' Cal asked him cheerfully as he walked up to them.

Theo looked almost murderous for a moment, and then muttered in his broken English accent, 'The men...the technicians have made an error. The lighting is not right.'

'So how long before we start filming this scene?' Kirsten asked, hoping she'd got time for a coffee.

'We'll run through it now.' Theo waved them towards the set. 'You sit on the bed, Kirsten; we'll go over the new lines.'

As she did as she was told Kirsten tried to ignore the way her heart was thudding unevenly against her chest.

Someone shoved a piece of paper into her hand and she tried to concentrate on the new lines that had been typed out for her.

You know I've always loved you, but this is impossible.

It was ironic that the line she had been struggling with was the first line they wanted her to deliver. She glared at it, willing herself to be calm, to get into character.

'OK—from the top.' Theo nodded over at Cal.

Kirsten watched him come into the room, walk over to the dressing table and deliver his lines perfectly. He was always such a damn perfectionist, she thought, so smugly self-assured. But she had to admit he was a skilful actor; he looked very much at home and at ease...and he also looked very good in that suit, she thought hazily; he was a very handsome man.

She suddenly realised that there was silence and everyone was waiting for her to speak.

'Sorry!' She glanced down at her sheet of paper, pulled herself very sharply together and delivered her lines.

'You know I've always loved you, but this is impossible.'

'Nothing is impossible, honey, if we just pull together.' Cal came and sat down next to her on the bed.

His thigh was touching against hers; she could feel the

heat of him burning through the delicate material of her nightdress. Suddenly she was reminded very forcibly of a night when Cal had come home and sat next to her like this and said words not dissimilar. Her mind blurred on the words she had to say next; her throat seemed to close over.

She heard Cal prompting her softly under his breath. 'I know we'll work this out...'

'I know we'll work this out,' she repeated.

Then he leaned closer, his lips coming within centimetres of hers. Her heart was beating so fiercely she felt sure he'd be able to hear it. She looked upwards into the vivid blue of his eyes and felt as if she was drowning. Abruptly she pulled away before he could touch her.

'How was that?' She looked wildly around for Theo. He was standing shaking his head, looking very annoyed. For an awful moment she thought he was about to tear into her, but to her relief she found he was looking beyond her at one of the technicians.

'Yes...all right.' He waved a hand dismissively. 'Go and get a coffee or something while I sort these lights out.'

Kirsten felt as if she'd had a reprieve from a death sentence.

'You OK?' Cal asked her as they walked together off the set.

'Of course I'm OK; why wouldn't I be?' she said defensively.

'I don't know...you just seemed on edge. You look very pale as well.' His eyes moved over her face with a kind of tender concern that tugged at her heartstrings.

'Well, I'm fine.' They stopped next to the coffee machine and she watched as he put a paper cup under the water.

'How's your dad?' he asked her suddenly.

'He's had the second lot of tests, we're just waiting for the results.' She took the hot coffee from him, noting that he'd remembered she drank it black with no sugar.

'If there's anything I can do, you'll let me know?'

'There's nothing any of us can do except wait.' Her voice held a faint tremor. How was it he could upset her more when he was being kind than when he was being infuriating? she wondered.

She looked down at her coffee and remembered a time when he had been wonderful to her...when they'd been happy. She frowned suddenly. She couldn't start thinking like that—it was a very slippery slope.

'Hell, this is awful coffee, almost as bad as the stuff you used to make,' Cal muttered, pulling a face.

'There's nothing wrong with the coffee I make,' she replied indignantly.

Cal smiled. 'You always made lousy coffee,' he said softly. 'Don't you remember your breakfast specialty...burnt coffee?'

She tried very hard not to smile at that memory. He was talking about the time during their first few days of marriage when she had put a coffee pot on the stove to keep warm and then got distracted...by him, as she recalled. She had to admit the coffee had tasted awful, but she had been too much in love at the time to care. Her eyes narrowed on him. 'No, I don't recall that.'

Behind them on set, Theo was doing a lot of shouting and arm waving. Kirsten turned to watch him, glad of the distraction.

'Where is Theo originally from?' she asked Cal as he also turned to watch what was going on.

'I don't know. I think he's part-Russian, part-Greek, apparently he speaks both languages fluently.'

'He's a bit fearsome, isn't he?' Kirsten reflected. 'But then, I've heard he's a genius and I suppose a lot of brilliant people are a bit eccentric.'

Cal smiled, but he didn't have time to answer because Theo had left the set and was marching towards them. 'We'll have to shoot another scene,' he said angrily. 'Nothing is right on there...nothing. And time is money.'

He stopped next to them, raking a hand through his hair with an air of absolute distraction. 'Come into my office, will you?' he ordered. 'There are a few things we need to talk about.' Then he marched on ahead of them towards a door at the end of the corridor.

Kirsten caught Cal's eye. 'What do you think he wants to talk to us about?' she whispered.

Cal gave a quizzical shrug and then grinned at her. Despite herself, she grinned back at him, then pulled herself up. What was she doing? Cal was not her friend and he was definitely not a co-conspirator. Turning away, she followed Theo down the hall.

Theo's office was tiny, almost like a broom cupboard. There was just room for his desk, two chairs and a filing cabinet. Cal stood just inside the door while Kirsten took the vacant chair opposite the director.

'OK…I just want to run through the details of filming next week.' Theo was rifling through the untidy piles of paper on his desk as he spoke. 'You know we are transferring to San Francisco; the locations manager has found a house that we will use for filming.'

Kirsten settled back into her chair, feeling a little more relaxed now that it was apparent Theo wasn't going to talk about adding sex scenes to the film. She knew all about the move to San Francisco; she'd been told when she accepted the part.

'Ah…here we are.' Theo found a piece of paper and pushed it towards her. 'That's just a rough schedule of the scenes we will be working on day by day.'

Kirsten glanced down at the paper, wondering how accurate it would be when the scene they were supposed to be working on today had been changed twice already.

'The studio will be providing accommodation for you in San Francisco, so you don't need to worry about that. My assistant will give you the details at the end of the week when she issues you with your flight tickets.'

There was silence and, thinking the meeting was now at a close, Kirsten started to get up.

'One last thing.' Kirsten sat back down as Theo started to rifle through the papers again. 'The PR people have been in contact with me this morning. They brought this to my attention.'

To Kirsten's horror, Theo brought out a magazine from the depths of the chaos...the same magazine that Chloe had been at pains to show her this morning.

Theo slid it across the table; it was open at the picture of her and Cal leaving Charlie's restaurant.

'Let me tell you right now that there is absolutely no truth in that article whatsoever.' Kirsten sat forward on her chair and looked over at Cal. 'It's complete rubbish...isn't it, Cal?'

'What is it?' Cal reached over her and picked up the magazine. 'Nice picture of you, Kirsten,' he murmured lazily. 'You're very photogenic, you know.'

'Never mind that. Will you please tell Theo that the article is rubbish? We were just having lunch—'

'I can't think why Theo would be interested.' Cal put the magazine down.

'I'm not,' Theo replied. 'It's the PR people that want me to draw it to your attention. They like this kind of thing...it will help sell the film. Sue Williams says she wants to come down to talk about it with you. Set up some interviews. I think she wants to do that in San Francisco—'

'Sue Williams?' Kirsten shook her head. 'Who—?'

'She's in charge of the PR department. Anyway...' Theo ruffled through the papers on his desk again '...they've asked me to tell you to play up this angle...this question...that there might be a rekindling of your romance. The publicity will be good; our film will keep getting a plug. Everyone will be happy.'

'Well, I'm not happy,' Kirsten said quickly. 'In fact, I'm

furious. There is no truth in that story. Cal and I are not getting back together—'

'It doesn't matter if it's true or not,' Theo said patiently. 'It's just a publicity stunt. If you've got any complaints, take it up with Sue…she should be dealing with this, not me. In the meantime they want you and Cal to attend a première together.' He reached under the papers and drew out an envelope. 'Here we are. It's on Saturday night. The studio have asked that you pick Kirsten up at around seven-thirty, Cal, and they want you to attend the party after the film and then take Kirsten home about midnight—'

'And do we have to go to bed together as well?' Kirsten asked scathingly. 'Cocoa at twelve-fifteen and satin pyjamas off by twelve-thirty?'

Theo's eyebrows rose. 'They haven't made any suggestions as to what happens after midnight—'

'I think that's when Kirsten turns into a pumpkin,' Cal put in drolly.

Kirsten shot him a look of annoyance. 'Well, at least I'm not going to turn into a rat like you—'

'Now, now!' Theo interjected warningly. 'We must have a good working relationship here.'

Kirsten shook her head angrily. 'Work is here at the studio; this is encroaching on my private life. Besides, I'm already going to that première, but I'm attending with Jason Giles.'

Theo shrugged. 'That's up to you. But the people upstairs won't be happy…there's a lot of money riding on this film and they will expect you to be co-operative.'

The implied threat hung heavily in the air. Kirsten stared at Theo. Did he mean if she was difficult that the studio would just refuse to work with her in the future?

'But this isn't right…' Kirsten looked around at Cal, hoping that he might support her. 'We are not going to do this, are we, Cal?'

He met her eyes steadily and shrugged. 'I've had to do

worse things for PR. I've no real objection to posing for a few photographs or ferrying you backwards and forwards to a première. I draw the line at the cocoa, though…I hate cocoa.'

Kirsten's eyes glittered a bright, intense green. She might have known that he wouldn't back her up.

'OK, that's settled.' Theo got up from his desk and put an envelope into Cal's hand. 'That's your invitations for Saturday. Let's get back to work now.'

Theo strode out of the room, leaving Kirsten staring at Cal with ill-disguised fury. 'What does he mean…that's settled? I haven't agreed to anything.'

'It's not really a big deal. You were going to go to that première anyway.' Cal shrugged.

'Yes, with Jason—'

'I'm sure Jason will get over the disappointment,' Cal said wryly. 'But it doesn't sound like the studio will. I'll pick you up at seven-thirty Saturday.' He turned to leave and then looked back at her. 'By the way…I was only joking about the cocoa,' he said with a grin. 'It's the pyjamas that I hate. I'd much prefer you in the outfit you're wearing now.'

CHAPTER THREE

THEY were in Kirsten's bedroom amidst chaos. The dressing table was cluttered with a wild assortment of jars, make-up and face creams, all in aid of Kirsten's last-minute effort to look her best, and the bed was strewn with Chloe's hairdressing equipment.

She'd planned to wear a long red dress to the première tonight. But that was when she had thought she was going with Jason. Her change of escort had thrown her into a total panic, and at the last minute she'd changed her mind about the red dress, rejecting it for being too daring. If it weren't for Chloe's kind offer to do her hair and help her get ready she would probably be really on the last minute by now, she thought.

'Thanks for helping, Chloe,' she said. 'I did think, right up to last night, that I'd be able to get out of this ridiculous charade. I've tried to ring Sue Williams all week but each time I've been told she is unavailable and will ring me back but she never does. Of course, if it had been Cal phoning she would have snapped to attention. But Cal didn't bother to phone her. Oh, no, Mr Cal McCormick could never be that decent. I swear he's just going along with all this to annoy me.'

'Hold still, for heaven's sake!' Chloe muttered, pushing Kirsten's head further forward so that she could stick a few more hairgrips in the back of her hair.

'The studio wouldn't want to fall out with Cal. So if he had backed me up I'm sure they would have dropped the idea.'

'Look on the bright side,' Chloe mumbled through a

mouthful of grips. 'A lot of women would love to be seen
on Cal McCormick's arm. It won't harm your career.'

'No…just my mental health. I've had the most awful
week with him at that studio, Chloe; you wouldn't believe
how irritating he can be. And tomorrow we have to go to
San Francisco together, because the studio has booked us
on the same flight. It's just the last straw having to go out
with him tonight as well.'

'But you used to love him once…didn't you?' Chloe said
softly. 'He can't be all bad.'

'No…he's not all bad,' Kirsten admitted. She could feel
her heart slamming against her chest as she thought about
that question. 'I did love him once…but it was a terrible
mistake.'

'So what were his good points?' Chloe asked, trying to
take her friend's mind off the evening ahead.

'I don't know.' Kirsten frowned; she didn't want to think
about his good points. She glanced sideways at the untidy
room. 'He was fanatically tidy.'

'That's not a good point.' Chloe stuck the last of the
grips in Kirsten's hair. 'There,' she said with a certain
amount of pleasure, 'you can look now.'

Kirsten looked up and met her reflection in her dressing-
table mirror in surprise. 'Wow! Is that really me?' She
watched as Chloe lifted up a mirror to show her the back.
She had wound her hair up into a very sophisticated chi-
gnon, which made Kirsten look extremely stylish and very
feminine. 'You've done a fantastic job, Chloe. Thank you.
And my make-up is great too!'

'I should have stuck to being a beautician, shouldn't I?'
Chloe smiled. 'At least I can make money out of that, unlike my acting career.'

Kirsten turned around to look at her friend. 'Didn't you
get that part you auditioned for?'

Chloe shook her head. 'I start back to work at the beauty
shop next Monday.'

Kirsten regarded her sympathetically. 'I'm so sorry, Chloe.'

Chloe shrugged. 'I've got another audition tomorrow…so, who knows? I might get lucky. And at least I like my job at the beauty shop. It could be worse.'

'Yes…like the job I got once as a singing waitress on rollerblades.'

'I remember you telling me about that.' Chloe laughed. 'Was that around the time you first went out with Cal?'

'No, I was successfully established as a singer when I first met Cal. Whereas his career in acting was just starting to take off.'

She was silent for a moment as she thought about that. 'Things seemed so uncomplicated back then. He used to make me laugh…we had such fun together.'

'So he did have some good points.'

'Just a few,' Kirsten admitted cautiously. She glanced at her wristwatch. 'He'll be here to pick me up soon. Are you sure I look all right?' She stood up from the dressing table so that Chloe could run a critical eye over her.

She was wearing a long white dress with shoestring straps that crossed provocatively low on her back. The material was finest silk and it clung to her figure before falling to the floor with a side split that showed a glimpse of long leg. 'You don't think it's too revealing?'

Chloe shook her head. 'You look stunning.' She tapped her fingers on the glossy magazines that she had brought with her into Kirsten's room. 'Just have a flick through these…they're all wearing dresses like that to the premières now.'

The shrill ring of the doorbell cut through the silence of the apartment. Kirsten looked at her friend in alarm. 'If that's him he's early!'

'Keep him waiting, then,' Chloe said, turning for the door. 'I'll go and let him in.'

Kirsten sat back down at the dressing table. She felt incredibly nervous, as if she had first-night jitters or something. This was a ridiculous situation, she thought angrily. Whoever had heard of being forced to date your ex-husband for publicity purposes? Hollywood was a weird place.

She heard Cal's voice from the hallway and stared down at her hands…hands now devoid of the wedding ring she had once worn. 'You must have loved him once.' The words echoed through her mind.

She had thought she loved him…had thought that it was love at first sight.

They had met at a wedding. She had been a friend of the bride; he'd been a friend of the groom. She had glanced across the aisle of the church and their eyes had met. Right there and then she had fallen under his spell.

He had looked so handsome in his dark suit, and when he'd smiled at her she had felt herself blush to the roots of her hair. She remembered feeling pleased that she had been wearing a wide-brimmed hat so that she could dip her head and hide from his deeply provocative gaze.

'Who's that?' she had whispered to her friend Charlotte, who had been sitting next to her. 'No…don't look yet… he'll know I'm asking about him.'

Charlotte had peeped from under her own hat and then smiled. 'That's Cal McCormick…he's an actor. He had a cameo role in the movie that made it big last summer. Apparently he's very up-and-coming. According to the grapevine, definitely one to watch.'

'I can agree with that.' Kirsten had smiled and risked another glance across the aisle. 'Who is he with?' she had asked, looking at the attractive brunette by his side.

'Maeve Ryan. She's married to Brian Harris, the director. He's a lot older than her, but apparently it's been a match made in heaven as far as her acting career is concerned. I think Brian is working abroad; that's why she's here with Cal. They're very good friends.'

They'd been more than just good friends, Kirsten thought

angrily now. Trouble was, she had been too blind to see it, and by the time she'd woken up to the fact she and Cal had been married, and she had been seven months pregnant.

The baby wasn't something Kirsten allowed herself to think about. It was too painful. Even now when her thoughts flitted over the subject she felt the raw thrust of emotion…a pain that had never healed.

She heard Chloe's laughter emanating from the living room. Obviously Mr Smooth was working his charms again, she thought. She glanced at her watch and stood up. Might as well get this over with.

Cal stood up as soon as she entered the room.

He looked incredible in a dark suit that most probably had a designer label; a white shirt open at the collar emphasised the tan of his skin and the darkness of his hair.

'You look lovely, Kirsten,' he said, his gaze moving leisurely over her figure with a gleam of male appreciation.

'Thanks.' She avoided his blue eyes, her senses were in enough disarray as it was, and instead she looked pointedly at her watch. 'I suppose if we are to stick to the studio's timetable we should be going.' She couldn't resist reminding him that she wasn't going out with him by choice.

'Yes, you're right,' he replied, totally unconcerned. He smiled over at Chloe. 'It's been a real pleasure meeting you.'

Kirsten watched her level-headed twenty-eight-year-old friend blush like a schoolgirl and cringed. It really wasn't fair that Cal had been given such power over women…such good looks.

'Have a wonderful evening,' Chloe said as they went out towards the front door.

'We'll try our best,' Cal replied and, catching Kirsten's eye, he grinned. 'But we're not promising anything.'

Cal wasn't too hot on promises, Kirsten thought sarcastically.

Considering that it was only early March, it was a pleas-

ant evening, warm and muggy with not a flicker of a breeze.
Kirsten settled herself into Cal's impressive sports car and
tried to count her blessings. No breeze to disturb her
hair…no wedding ring…no complications in her life. Once
the première was over and they got to the party she would
ditch Cal until it was time to go home.

'How did good ol' Jason take being stood up?' Cal asked
as he stopped the car at some traffic lights.

'As you can imagine, he wasn't pleased. But I told him
I'd see him there, and have a drink with him at the party.'

'He's still going, then?'

'Of course.'

She hesitated and then found the courage to ask, 'And
what about you? Will your current girlfriend be there?'

'Which current girlfriend are you talking about?' He
grinned at her, a spark of devilment in his eyes.

'Still putting it about, then,' she muttered. 'Some things
don't change.'

'I'm a single guy, Kirsten. There is nothing to stop me
putting it about, as you so quaintly like to put it.'

What about Maeve, Kirsten wanted to ask, doesn't she
ever get a bit jealous? She bit back the words, some things
were best left unsaid.

'At least as neither of us is seriously involved with anyone no one is going to be hurt by what's written in the
papers about us,' Cal continued.

'Speak for yourself,' Kirsten said in annoyance, and then
found herself lying. 'Actually Jason's fizzing.'

'So the relationship is serious, then?'

'I told you, Jason and I are very close.'

'Well, forgive me if I don't lose sleep over Jason. I really
couldn't care if he's annoyed or not.'

'I wouldn't expect you to care.' Kirsten stared out at the
dark sidewalks and wondered why the heck she felt im-
pelled to lie about her relationship with Jason. He'd been
disappointed when she'd cancelled, but she couldn't hon-

estly say he'd been annoyed. Was she so damn proud that she couldn't bear for Cal to know that there was nobody serious in her life? Hadn't been since the divorce?

Up ahead, Kirsten could see the theatre floodlit against the night sky, and she started to prepare herself mentally for the flash of photographers' bulbs and the onslaught of media attention.

The entrance to the theatre was roped off to keep the crowds at bay. As each car drew up and celebrities walked up along the red-carpeted area there were cheers and whistles from the perimeters. Being basically shy, Kirsten hated these events. She was OK being the centre of attention when she was playing a part, or when she was lost in her music, but these occasions where she was just herself with no work to hide behind really threw her. She still couldn't believe that anyone would be interested in what she had to say, or what she was doing with her life. It was a complete mystery to her.

'You still hate these things, don't you?' Cal threw her a sympathetic look as he started to slow the car, and she found herself remembering the many times in the past when he had supported her through promotion events, always there with a gentle word of encouragement, a protective arm around her waist. That had been the one good thing about being married to him, she remembered suddenly. He'd always shielded her from potential problems, eased the way with his charm and his confidence.

'I'm fine.' She angled her chin high, determined not to let him see that the shy country girl still existed. 'They don't cause me a second thought any more.'

'Good.' He smiled and pulled the car to a halt. Then they were stepping out into the media circus. For a second Kirsten was blinded by the amount of cameras that flashed in their direction.

Cal's car was driven away by the valet parking attendant and he walked to her side.

'Cal...over here...over here.' Various journalists and photographers vied with each other for his attention.

He smiled and then, putting a gentle hand against her back, guided her up towards the theatre entrance. She couldn't help comparing this to the times when she had arrived here with Jason. There had never been this flurry of excitement...this level of interest zoomed in on every smile, every exchange between them. Kirsten hadn't experienced this since the days when Cal had been her husband and his career had suddenly rocketed upwards.

'Cal, have you got a moment? This is Sandy Peterson, for Cable TV.' A glamorous blonde stopped them just beside the door of the theatre.

'Would you mind giving a quick interview for tomorrow's *Hot News* programme?'

'Just for you,' Cal agreed with a grin.

Kirsten was very conscious of the way he pulled her closer to him as he spoke to the other woman, she was aware of his hand resting against the naked skin of her back, could feel the warmth of him pressed against her.

'Could you tell us a little bit about the film *The Love Child* that you are currently working on?' The cameras moved closer.

'It's a modern love story about a couple who are married but have no children. They love each other, but somewhere along the way that's been forgotten amid the pressure of their high-flying careers. Then unexpectedly they are asked to look after Henry, their six-year-old nephew, and his dog, and that's when a well-ordered lifestyle starts to fall out of shape.'

'That part is being played by Josh Summers, isn't it?' Sandy intercepted.

'That's right.'

Sandy smiled and her attention turned to Kirsten. 'Now, you play the part of Cal's wife, Helen. Is this a familiar feeling for you...after all, you used to play the part in real life, didn't you? You and Cal were married for nearly a year.'

'It's come as a bit of a surprise, finding myself acting alongside Cal,' Kirsten admitted. 'They say never work with animals or children. I think they should add ex-husbands to the list, then I'll have a hat trick.' She smiled.

'Do you think the more serious aspects of this story reflect in any way your marriage break-up in real life with Cal?'

Kirsten was totally unprepared for that question.

'Now, Sandy, we can't answer that,' Cal cut in smoothly to the rescue. 'Kirsten and I have moved on from the past. That's why we can work so well together now. But the film we are shooting is basically light-hearted. It's about not taking things for granted…it's about two adults whose priorities are sharply jogged back into place by a child.'

'And is there any truth in the rumour that you two are getting back together?'

'We are going to plead the fifth on that, aren't we, sweetheart?' Cal gazed down at Kirsten with warmth in his eyes and she felt her insides melt. 'Let's just say we are taking things a day at a time, but it feels real good being here together tonight.'

'Have you anything to add to that?' Sandy asked, moving the microphone towards Kirsten again.

Kirsten could hardly think straight because Cal's fingers were stroking against her skin caressingly and the feeling was sending shivery, sensuous sensations shooting through her.

She didn't dare make a scene but she really wanted to pull away from him. 'We're just good friends,' she managed to murmur.

'Very good friends.' Cal bent closer and before she realised his intentions he kissed her softly on the lips. The kiss was over almost before it had begun but not before it had rocked Kirsten's tenuous composure. Her body felt as if someone had just lit a bonfire in it.

There was a whistle of approval from the watching crowds, then they were moving swiftly on inside the theatre.

'Wasn't too bad, was it?' Cal asked her in a low tone against her ear as they entered the foyer.

'Are you joking?' she breathed unsteadily. 'It was a nightmare. How dare you kiss me like that?'

'Nothing personal,' he replied. 'Just doing my good-deeds act for the PR people.'

Kirsten felt anger sizzling all the way through her, even into her toes. Before she could formulate any kind of a reply, however, they were walking through towards the auditorium.

She saw Jason across the crowds and he waved. She waved back and felt a tinge of regret that she wasn't sitting with him. Jason was such undemanding 'safe' company. They'd chat about the film they were about to see, and he'd have all the behind-the-scenes gossip, but more importantly whenever he accidentally brushed against her there was no wave of sensual awareness, no undercurrent of dangerous passion. Not like now with Cal.

As they took their seats she was painfully aware of everything about him. She could feel the soft material of his jacket pressed against her bare arm. Could smell the familiar tang of his aftershave. She tried to make herself as small as possible in her chair so that there was no possibility of touching, but in the confined space she was fighting a losing battle.

The lights went down and the music started to play. Cal leaned closer and whispered against her ear. 'Theo will be here tonight with his new bride; apparently she is a stunning beauty.'

Kirsten shivered at the unexpected closeness, at the sensation of his breath against sensitive skin. All her senses were so tuned into him that she couldn't concentrate on the credits of the movie at all.

'Are you warm enough?' Cal asked as he casually draped a hand around the back of her. 'The air-conditioning is a bit fierce, isn't it?'

She wanted to pull away from him, but there was no room. She felt trapped…and overwhelmed by memories of other occasions when they had sat close together like this, Cal whispering in her ear, a sense of warmth and togetherness flowing easily between them.

Kirsten tried hard to concentrate on the lists of names that flashed before her eyes on the big screen. Tried very hard to concentrate on what was being said, but inside her mind there was a different set of pictures unfolding…none of them welcome.

She was remembering the first time Cal had kissed her beneath a shimmering full moon. Behind them the sounds of the wedding party in full flow.

They had hardly known each other, hardly exchanged more than a few sentences, but when he'd folded her into his arms the emotional freefall had been spectacular.

She had never met anyone who could seduce her with just a smile or a certain gleam in his eye. Her normal caution, her usual rules had all been swept aside. They had slept together on their third date, and even trying to maintain the will power to wait that long had been difficult.

He'd invited her to his apartment for dinner. But they had never got around to eating the food he'd prepared. Several hours later they had lain languidly in each other's arms, naked bodies pressed close together in the afterglow of love, other appetites forgotten.

She remembered that same evening she had learnt that her record had just gone into the top ten in the charts.

Things had just seemed too good to be true…and of course they had been.

It was only after the wedding day that the cracks had

started to appear in their relationship and the doubts had started. Had Cal married her because he loved her, or because she was two months pregnant?

On the day of their wedding she had firmly believed it was love, but as time unfolded that certainty had diminished and dwindled to a mere spark of hope.

A lot of the problem had been down to the stress of their careers. They'd constantly been pulled in opposite directions. For the first few months of their marriage Cal had been filming on location in the Caribbean and Kirsten had been in New York, plugging a new record.

When they had got back together Cal had told her that once the baby was born he wanted them to go to London, where he'd been offered a major deal in a movie that was going to be very big. She hadn't been too keen because she'd hoped that once the baby was a few months old she could record a new album at the LA recording studios.

A conflict of careers had ensued. Hers versus his. And the atmosphere between them had been heated. But, although they'd argued, when Cal had taken her into his arms and held her at night she'd known deep in her heart that she would give in, that she would follow him to the ends of the earth if need be. Naïvely she had believed that their only problems were work-related...and that they could be overcome.

Then, when she'd been seven months pregnant, she had discovered the real reason Cal was so keen on the acting job in England...his co-star was to be Maeve.

Maeve had coolly informed her of this one night at a dinner party, had more or less insinuated that Kirsten was responsible for keeping them apart. 'We're very special to each other, Kirsten,' she had said meaningfully. 'I hope you understand this?'

'No, I don't understand, Maeve,' she replied quickly. 'What are you trying to say?'

'Just that of course Cal loves you...you're the mother of

his expected child.' Maeve's tone was patronising. 'And of course that makes you special—after all, it's why he married you... But Cal and I also have a very special relationship. Don't ever forget that.'

The sheer audacity of the words blew Kirsten's mind, and suddenly huge, distasteful chunks of a jigsaw started to fall into place.

'How do you feel about Maeve?' she asked Cal on the way home.

He slanted a rather odd look at her. 'What do you mean, how do I feel about her?'

'Would you describe her as special?' she persisted.

He thought about that for a moment, and then inclined his head. 'Yes, I suppose I would.' Then he reached for her hand and added lightly, 'Not as special as the mother of my baby, of course.'

They were the wrong words at the wrong moment. She didn't want him to love her just because she was the mother of his forthcoming child. It wasn't enough... She had never been a jealous person, but that night she felt the first pangs of the emotion and they hurt deeply.

Maybe they would have worked things out...maybe she would have kept Cal if their baby had lived. He'd been so very keen on being a father and he might have chosen her and the baby over Maeve... She had spent many nights wondering about that afterwards...thinking about what might have been.

But once they had lost the baby, suddenly everything had been wrong. Even the nights when they had lain together in the same large double bed had been spent stiffly apart. By day they had thrown themselves into their work with gusto, and to outward appearances they had both seemed to cope well with the tragedy, but what they had really been doing was using work as a means of escape. In reality their marriage had been over.

The lights in the theatre started to go up, startling Kirsten back to awareness.

'What did you think?' Cal asked as he took his arm away from her, and she realised with embarrassment that the film was over and she hadn't seen any of it.

'It was OK.' She blinked in the bright lights.

'Are you all right?' Cal glanced at her in concern.

'Of course.' Very quickly she tried to pull herself together. Cal was too damned perceptive sometimes and she would die rather than let him know that she was anything other than perfectly in control.

He looked at her with disbelief. 'What was it that got to you…was it the part where the dog died? You're always a sucker when it comes to animals.'

She smiled shakily. Thank heavens there was something in the film that warranted a tear, Kirsten thought grimly, unable to believe that she had sat all the way through a film without seeing a thing! She really was going to have to forget the past before it ruined her future.

'No, I've just got something in my eye.' Kirsten stood up briskly as everyone got to their feet. She couldn't wait to get out of here.

'Would you like to give the party a miss?' Cal asked once they were outside in the warmth of the evening.

'What about the studio and our timetable?'

Cal shrugged. 'The studio might forgive us if we go somewhere intimate and have supper.'

'I'm not hungry,' Kirsten answered quickly, the thought of being alone with him in an intimate setting giving her immediate palpitations. 'Anyway, I said I'd meet Jason at the party for a drink.'

'We mustn't disappoint Jason then,' Cal said drily, opening the passenger door of his car for her.

The party was like most of the others Kirsten had attended in Hollywood; an occasion for networking, for seeing who exactly was in the upper echelons of the movie business and who was to be avoided. It was all incredibly false. The only thing in its favour was the champagne and the venue, which was one of Los Angeles's premier hotels.

Kirsten stood by the window and looked out over the glittering skyline of the city. She could hear a woman behind her talking to a producer, gushing with enthusiasm about how wonderful his film was, how brilliantly cast. Then as he left to talk to someone else she could hear her saying in a derisory tone, 'The best actor in it was the dog.'

Kirsten looked over and caught Cal's eye and they both laughed. For a second Kirsten felt the tension that had been eating her all evening lessen. In that instant they were transported back to a time when they had laughed easily together, both on the same wavelength with the same sense of humour.

'I told you we should have skipped this party,' Cal said, reaching to get her another glass of champagne from a passing waiter. 'I knew it would be full of flakes.'

'Yeah, but you love it really, don't you?' she murmured sardonically.

'No, I don't,' he said quietly. 'I'd have much preferred to be alone with you a million miles away from here.'

Kirsten met his eyes with a feeling of uncertainty. There were times when he totally confounded her. Was he just being charming because he wanted them to work well together? It seemed the most likely explanation.

Across the room she saw Jason making his way through the crowds. He smiled at her as their eyes met.

'Film was OK, wasn't it?' he said as he joined them. 'Hello, Kirsty.' He kissed her on the cheek and then turned his attention to Cal. 'Haven't seen you at one of these occasions for a while.'

'No, I think the last time was when you were here with Kirsten…just after we split up,' Cal replied.

'Was it?' Jason looked as if he didn't recall that event,

but Kirsten did. If ever she had needed Jason's moral support it had been that night. She remembered keeping her arm linked firmly through his, trying not to notice how many women approached Cal.

A group of people claimed Cal's attention and Jason took the opportunity to pull Kirsten to one side.

'How's it going?' he asked with concern.

'So far, so good.' Kirsten glanced back over at Cal, noticing how he was almost a head taller than most people in the room, including Jason.

Kirsten didn't want to compare the two men…after all, Jason was a really nice guy. And yet she did find herself measuring them against each other. They were about the same age, and, like Cal, Jason was wearing a stylish suit, but there the similarities ended. Jason's hair was thick and blond, maybe not even entirely natural-looking. His physique was lightweight compared to Cal's, in fact, his suit seemed to drop away at his shoulders instead of fitting them.

She wished suddenly that Jason could turn her on, excite her, the way Cal had once. Then she was ashamed of the thought. Cal was history.

'I'd like to take you home,' Jason said urgently, claiming her full attention back.

Kirsten shook her head. 'I can't; I'm stuck with Cal tonight.'

'You're bearing up under the strain anyway,' he murmured, an edge to his voice.

His tone took her aback a little, as did the way he was looking at her. Was Jason just a little bit jealous? she wondered suddenly. Then dismissed the notion. Jason had never been jealous before; they didn't have that kind of a relationship.

'I can assure you that appearances can be very deceptive,' she told him. 'This is all a charade for the PR people.

Which reminds me, have you ever heard of the production company, Sugar Productions?'

'No, can't say I have. Must be a new company.'

'Yes, they are. They're making this film that we are working on and I thought if I could talk to someone there about this PR stuff it might help. But there was no one available to talk to me.'

'It sounds like you're having a tough time. I'm sorry, Kirsten, if I sounded a bit on edge before…it's just that there was something I wanted to talk to you about and I was hoping I could do it tonight.'

Kirsten frowned and leaned closer to him. 'Is it something to do with work?' she whispered.

'It's…' Jason shook his head. 'It's not work. Just… something I would like to talk to you about.'

'I don't know when we can get together now; I'm going to San Francisco tomorrow and—'

'Listen, I've got to go up to San Francisco soon on business,' Jason said suddenly. 'How about if we meet then? Grab some supper together?'

'That sounds good.' Kirsten nodded. 'Phone me on my mobile and we'll arrange it.'

'Thanks.' For a fleeting second Jason touched her face with his hand. Kirsten wished she hadn't caught Cal's eye at that moment, the derision in his expression made her blush.

'Kirsten, I'm going to miss you, you know,' Jason said softly under his breath.

Kirsten smiled. 'I'll see you soon, Jason,' she reassured him, and he pulled her close and kissed her cheek.

'Sorry to break up your tender moment but I think we should be going, Kirsten,' Cal cut in on them abruptly. 'We've got an early start tomorrow, travelling to Frisco.'

'Yes…' Kirsten looked with concern at Jason. 'Are you OK?'

He nodded and reluctantly released his hold. Then, with

a curt nod at Cal, he made his way over to mingle with the
crowds.

'Gives up easily, doesn't he?' Cal remarked drily.

'What do you mean?' she muttered.

'I heard him saying he wanted to take you home. Then
he just caved in.'

'Yeah, well, maybe the mighty weight of the PR moguls
got to him?' She arched a look of annoyance at him. 'And,
anyway, Jason isn't one to make a fuss. He's a gentleman.'

'Is that code for bad in bed?'

'You're disgusting sometimes.' Kirsten marched away
from him, her heart thudding unevenly against her chest as
she fought with herself to keep cool and not to create a
scene.

She didn't speak to him as they got outside.

'Jason always fancied you,' Cal continued, undeterred,
as they got back into his car. 'I don't care what you say
about him being so damned gentlemanly. As far as I'm
concerned, he lost no time in wrapping his arms around
you as soon as I walked out the front door.'

That wasn't true, but Kirsten didn't bother to argue the
point again. She had attended a première with Jason soon
after Cal had left her, but there had been nothing between
them except friendship. Jason had rung her out of sympathy
and to pay his respects when he heard about the loss of
their baby, and he had been so gentle and so understanding
that Kirsten had poured her heart out to him on the phone
and told him that Cal had just left.

She couldn't think back to that bleak time now without
a feeling of thanks for the support Jason had given her.

'I thought you'd be happily ensconced in a love nest
together by now...an engagement ring on your finger,' Cal
continued with a sardonic note in his voice.

'Just lay off Jason, OK?' she warned him edgily.

'Touched a nerve, have I? Doesn't he want to commit to
you—?'

'Mind your own business, Cal,' she said succinctly, refusing to rise to the bait.

'Only making conversation.' He shrugged.

What about you? she wanted to ask... Where was Maeve? Was he still hanging around, hoping she'd divorce her husband? But she wouldn't ask that question, she told herself, her resolve stiffening. She wouldn't lower herself; he might misinterpret and think she cared.

Cal pulled up outside her apartment. The streets were dark, and all the lights were out on her front porch.

Kirsten reached for the door handle of the car, anxious to escape.

'Aren't you forgetting something?' Cal asked her.

She hesitated and turned back with a frown. 'What?'

He nodded towards the clock on the dashboard. 'It's ten minutes to midnight. We've got time left over.'

She looked at him blankly, unable to read his expression in the darkness. 'What are you talking about—?'

Her words were effectively and firmly silenced as he bent closer and kissed her. Shock coursed through her. Unlike the kiss outside the première, this was no brief, controlled kiss, this was long and lingering and all-consuming. It caught Kirsten completely off-guard and off-balance and for a confusing second she found herself kissing him back, her stomach tying itself into a thousand knots of longing as she felt his hand touching against her face, holding and controlling her in a confident caress.

She was breathless as he released her. 'Why did you do that?' she asked shakily. 'There are no reporters about.'

'Aren't there?' She heard the smile in his voice and wished she could see his eyes properly. Was he laughing at her? Was this all just some huge joke to him?

'That wasn't a publicity stunt, Kirsten,' he drawled huskily. 'That was very much for old times' sake.'

CHAPTER FOUR

KIRSTEN dreamt about her baby that night. She saw her in cute dungarees, kicking her legs, laughing and gurgling, plump little arms outstretched as she waited to be lifted from her cot. She could see her so clearly, even the dimples in her fingers, and her eyes, big and blue like her father's.

The pillow was wet with her tears when she woke up and it took several moments to stop the sobs that racked her body.

She reached to put on the bedside lamp, and, blinking in its bright glare, wiped her face angrily. She hadn't had this dream for over six months. She had thought that it had gone away, that she was over the worst of this now.

She lay staring up at the ceiling and tried to switch her mind away from the little girl she had longed for. Bethany had been stillborn; she had never looked up and gurgled with delight. Kirsten didn't even know if her eyes had been blue like Cal's. For a second Kirsten's heart ached so much she felt it might break.

Pushing the covers back, she sat on the side of the bed.

This was all Cal's fault, she thought shakily. That kiss last night had thrown her body into chaos; it had stirred up memories that she wanted so much to forget. She didn't want to go with him to San Francisco today; she wanted to run in the opposite direction as far away as she could get.

The alarm clock said five-thirty. Next to it, propped up against the lamp, were the air tickets she had been given for San Francisco and the address and keys for the apartment that the studio were renting for her whilst she had to work there.

At the other side of the bedroom sat the two suitcases

that she had packed when she returned from the première last night. She hadn't been able to go straight to bed; she had been so wound up. As a result, everything was organised, her room was immaculately tidy, and a taxi was picking her up to catch her flight at nine-thirty.

She should really get back into bed and try and get some sleep. But, as tired as she was, she knew that there was no way she was going to be able to do that now, so she reached for her dressing gown and went downstairs to make herself a drink.

At least there was no work for two days; that would start bright and early on Tuesday morning when the rest of the crew were settled in San Francisco. She tried to console herself with this as she sat in the lounge and leafed through some of Chloe's magazines from the rack by the TV. Her intention was to take her mind off the past. But the first thing she saw when she opened the front cover of the magazine was another article about Cal and a picture of her and Cal on their wedding day.

Although the picture had been taken nearly three years ago she looked incredibly young in it—young and full of hope. Her eyes were shining, and she was smiling up at Cal as if she worshipped the ground he walked on, which she supposed she had done at the time. She'd certainly been infatuated by him. She studied the dress she had been wearing, a pale blue silk sheath, which skimmed her slender figure in a flattering way. No one would ever have guessed that she had been just over two months pregnant.

Cal was wearing a dark suit. It was harder to tell what was going through his mind in the photo. He looked coolly enigmatic, a small smile curving his lips, his arm lightly around her waist.

She had thought that he loved her. When she had told him that she was pregnant and he'd asked her to marry him she hadn't doubted for a second that he loved her. She had been blissfully happy and had believed he was too. But now when she looked at the photograph she wondered if in reality he had just felt trapped that day, because the woman he had really wanted to marry was Maeve, and she was unavailable.

Kirsten threw the magazine down; she was in no mood for this. Why did Chloe buy these rubbishy magazines? she wondered as she went back into the kitchen to make herself another drink.

She stared out of the back window. Dawn was breaking in the distance. She thought about the way Cal had kissed her last night and writhed inside with a mixture of desire and fear. The thing that really scared her was the way she had instinctively responded to him. She had thought that there was no way Cal McCormick would ever be able to turn her on like that again, and yet as soon as he touched her she had felt the same weakness, the same sizzling chemistry that had drawn her to him once before. She had thought she'd learnt her lesson there, had damned well hoped she had.

Her eyes moved from the vivid pink sky to her car sitting out on the street. It was at that moment she made the decision not to take the flight to San Francisco, but to drive instead.

Immediately she felt better. It should only take about six hours, all right, it was a heck of a lot longer than the short flight, but on the plus side she would have her own car whilst in San Francisco instead of having to rent one, plus she wouldn't have to travel with Cal. Anything that put off seeing Cal for forty-eight hours had to be a good plan, she thought wryly. She smiled to herself. She'd even be able to call and see her parents on the way up, have lunch with them.

She glanced at her watch. As soon as it got to a more civilised time of the morning she'd ring her parents and tell them to expect her, and she supposed she had better phone the studio as well, let them know her plans. Meanwhile she'd try and get some rest and set off after the rush-hour traffic cleared.

Kirsten and Chloe were just finishing a leisurely breakfast in the kitchen when the front doorbell rang. 'I'll get it,' Chloe said cheerfully.

Getting up to clear the dishes from the table, Kirsten heard her say hello to somebody. She sounded startled and Kirsten smiled to herself, thinking it was Chloe's boyfriend John. They'd had an argument last week but Kirsten suspected it was just a temporary glitch. John had probably come around to say sorry.

She was stunned when she turned from the dishwasher and saw that it wasn't John but Cal following Chloe back into the kitchen.

He was dressed casually yet very stylishly in beige trousers and a cream T-shirt and he looked very handsome.

'Morning, Kirsty.' He smiled easily at her as if it were quite normal for him to turn up at breakfast-time. As she met his eyes the memory of what had transpired between them last night was instantly there. She felt awareness and then embarrassment wash through her as his eyes then lowered and flicked over her appearance in a quick assessment.

Why did she wish suddenly that she had paid more attention to her appearance that morning? That she hadn't flung on the first thing that came to hand, a faded pair of denim jeans and a pale blue T-shirt, and left her hair loose? She frowned. Why should she care? It was of no concern to her what Cal might think.

'What are you doing here?' she asked with a frown, shooting a glance at the kitchen clock. 'Shouldn't you be at the airport?'

'Yes, and I would be there except Theo rang me in a total panic a little while ago.'

'What's the matter with Theo?' Kirsten asked warily.

'Before I go into that, is there any more coffee in that

pot?' Cal asked, sliding out a chair from under the kitchen table and sitting down. He looked very much at home amidst the informal clutter of the kitchen and there was something about the way he was so relaxed that made Kirsten feel even more on edge.

She didn't move to pour him a coffee, but Chloe did. She got a cup and saucer out of the cupboard...one of their best bone-china ones, Kirsten noted drily. Then proceeded to pour Cal a cup whilst flicking an apologetic glance over at Kirsten.

'Thanks, Chloe.' Cal took a long, savouring sip of the black liquid, then grinned. 'Good coffee, I take it you didn't make it?' He shot Kirsten a glance.

The fact that he was correct in his assumption only made Kirsten's nerves fray even further. 'Cut to the point, Cal, will you?' she asked impatiently. 'What's wrong with Theo?'

'He's pretty upset with you.' Cal moved his chair so that he could stretch his long legs out. 'Livid, in fact.'

'Livid?' She frowned. 'Why, what have I done?'

'He wanted you on that flight this morning. There were a few things he wanted to run through with us.'

'But the studio said it was OK when I phoned there—'

'Whoever told you that is in trouble. Theo is not a happy man.'

Kirsten flicked another apprehensive glance at the clock on the wall. 'I won't make the flight now. It's cutting it too close. Can't he go through these notes with me tomorrow?'

'No, he's tied up in a meeting tomorrow with the location people. But it's all right.' Cal shrugged. 'Theo ran through a few of his ideas with me, and he's given me his notes. I said I'd drive down to San Francisco with you and we can run through them together on the way. I said we'd work on them tomorrow as well. It seemed to pacify him.'

'You said what?' Kirsten stared at him in horror. Why couldn't he leave her alone to make her own arrangements?

'It's OK, you don't need to thank me,' Cal said with a grin.

As for thanking him, she would rather have spent six hours driving with Theo frothing from the mouth than spend the time with Cal. This was like some kind of bad dream, where Cal kept turning up over and over again to torment her. 'But it's a long drive and I...'

'I know, it's a damn nuisance. Why the heck did you decide not to fly?'

She wanted to tell him straight, that a six-hour drive had seemed preferable to even one hour in his company. But she held her tongue. Flinging insults at him at this stage wasn't going to help. 'I wanted to call and see my parents,' she said instead.

'Oh!' His face cleared. 'Well, I wouldn't mind seeing Robert and Lynn again.'

'You must be joking!' That was the point where Kirsten lost her cool.

Chloe cleared her throat. 'Er...if you'll excuse me. I'm going to go and have a shower. I've got an audition in an hour.' Kirsten glanced over at her friend and realised she was diplomatically leaving them to it.

'Yes, thanks, Chloe, and listen, break a leg today, OK?'

'Yeah.' Chloe grinned and slanted a look at Cal. 'You too,' she said softly.

There was silence for a moment when they were left alone.

Cal glanced at his watch. 'If we are going to make a detour down to see your parents we'd better get a move on.'

'Cal, I am not taking you to see my parents,' she said firmly, her voice steadier now.

'Why not?' He frowned.

'Because....' She shook her head helplessly. 'Look, I

shouldn't have to explain this to you. It's common sense. You and I are divorced. My parents won't want to see you.'

Cal looked genuinely perplexed by this. 'Why not?'

Kirsten slapped the flat of her hand against her forehead. 'I've just told you. We're divorced—'

'I think Lynn and Robert might have figured that out by now.'

'Don't get smart, Cal—' Her voice shook. 'I'm not having you upsetting my parents again.'

'I've never fallen out with your parents,' Cal said gently. 'I like and respect them very much.'

Kirsten swallowed hard. Why did she feel like crying suddenly? 'Yes, well, that may be the case,' she said in a low, trembling tone. 'But…but you still hurt them.'

Cal got up from the table. 'I know our divorce was a grim time for them,' he said quietly. 'But, unlike you, Kirsten, they still like me enough to look on me as a friend.'

Kirsten stared at him. 'How come you are so certain of that?' she asked, her tone raw.

'Just after we split up they sent me a very thoughtful and understanding letter and they still send me Christmas cards.'

Kirsten couldn't have been more surprised had he told her that her father was a secret agent for the FBI.

'They didn't tell me they were in contact with you,' she said.

Cal's eyes met hers. 'Why do you think that was?'

'I don't know.' She shrugged.

'I still have the letter. I'll show it to you some time if you'd like. It's very touching…and extremely perceptive—'

'No, thanks, I'll pass on that.' She glared at him.

Cal watched her for a moment. 'Kirsten, maybe I wasn't the best husband in the world,' he said gently, 'but it wasn't my fault that Bethany died.'

The words reverberated through Kirsten like a time bomb. 'I don't want to talk about…that.' She stopped him, her voice tightly controlled, her face ashen. She didn't want to discuss it with him…couldn't discuss it with him.

He seemed about to argue, to say something else, then his gaze moved over her stricken features and he shrugged. 'OK.' He glanced up at the kitchen clock. 'We should be going. I take it those are your suitcases in the hallway?'

She nodded, relieved beyond words that the subject was changed.

'If you give me your car keys, I'll put them in the trunk.'

She went to get her handbag, noting as she passed that another suitcase now sat next to hers in the hallway. 'Where's your car?'

'I took a cab over here.'

Silently she handed him her car keys.

'Are you ready to leave?' Cal asked, heading for the doorway.

'Just give me a minute.'

He nodded and turned to deal with the cases. As soon as the front door closed behind him Kirsten wanted to run and lock it. She wanted to shout childishly after him, Go away and don't come back. Instead she schooled herself to go upstairs and tidy herself up.

She brushed her hair and tied it back in a pony-tail, then applied some lipstick to brighten herself up. But she was just going through the motions because inside she felt numb.

She remembered feeling like this when her marriage had been falling apart. She'd still been reeling from losing Bethany and she just hadn't been able to cope emotionally with any of it. She had felt raw, yet detached from everything, as if it was all somehow unreal and happening to somebody else. Somehow she had managed to pull herself back from the brink, and she had got over it.

Now with Cal coming back into her life she felt suddenly

as if she had returned to square one. All the old pain was back...all the feeling of shocked disbelief...even the dreams, and he was as detached as ever.

Her eyes moved to the telephone in her bedroom. And hurriedly she went across to phone her parents to tell them she wouldn't be coming for lunch today after all. Maybe what Cal had said was true. Maybe her parents had written to him, had put the divorce and what had happened behind them. But, even if that was the case, Kirsten couldn't hack a reunion between Cal and her parents. It was another step backwards down a road that was too painful even to contemplate.

She dialled the number and waited but the number was engaged. As she waited for the line to clear she walked with the receiver to the window and looked idly out.

Cal was leaning against her car in the bright morning sunshine. He was talking to someone on his mobile phone.

Come on, Mum, who the heck are you talking to? Kirsten urged, turning away from the window.

Then abruptly she got through, but, although she allowed it to ring and ring, no one answered.

Maybe they had both gone out immediately they'd hung up from the last call. They were probably both on their way into town, happily planning what they were going to cook for lunch for her. Or maybe her mother was vacuuming and couldn't hear the phone.

They were going to be so disappointed when she told them she wasn't coming. But it couldn't be helped...with the best will in the world she couldn't go now.

'Kirsten, are you ready?' Cal called from the hall.

'Yes...coming.' She put the receiver down. She'd just have to try and phone them later in the morning.

'If you want to drive to my house we can transfer the cases to my car and I'll drive,' Cal suggested when she joined him outside.

'No, I want to drive, thank you.' She got behind the wheel. 'I want my car whilst I'm in San Francisco.'

'You can always rent one. Which is what I intended to do.'

'I'd rather drive my own.'

'Formed some kind of emotional attachment to the old jalopy, have you?'

Kirsten remembered his stylish car with the dashboard like an aeroplane and heated leather seats. She supposed her vehicle did seem like an old jalopy compared to his. 'It might be old,' she said tightly, 'but it's perfectly adequate for me.'

At least they were back to backbiting about nothing, she thought. She could just about handle that. It was when the conversation skidded off into deeper, more specific details that she felt overwhelmed by emotions that truly terrified her.

'Do you want me to drive?' he asked.

She gave a forced smile. He was doing it again, trying to take over. 'What's the matter, don't you like being chauffeured by a woman?' She slanted a wry glance at him.

'On the contrary, I quite like it,' he smiled. 'I was just being chivalrous.'

'That will be the day.'

Kirsten looked at the road stretching ahead. She was driving along the coast; the sky was a cloudless, dazzling blue and the sun glittered on the ocean like silver raindrops. She felt her heart lift. It was a perfect spring day. If she ignored Cal and concentrated on her driving the time should pass quickly. It would be OK, she'd handle it, and it would give her the chance to show him how little he meant to her now. Then the scenes in the film would be easier; he'd know she was only acting.

'Shouldn't you have turned right there?' Cal asked her.

She shook her head. 'Don't be a backseat driver, Cal. I've looked at the map; I know which way I'm going.'

Cal shrugged.

She was aware suddenly that instead of looking out of the windows he was watching her. She tried to pretend that she didn't notice, but it was unnerving. Why was he staring at her like that? Did she have a mark on her face? Maybe her mascara was smudged? She desperately wanted to check her reflection in the mirror, but didn't dare take her eyes off the road.

'I'm sure you should have turned there,' Cal said again.

'Shouldn't you be running through Theo's notes?' She flashed him an impatient look.

'OK.' He reached onto the back seat and lifted up a folder.

There was silence for a while as he leafed through them.

'Right…the scene we shot yesterday, where we are at breakfast, Theo flicked through the rushes early this morning and he thinks that you're not looking at me enough.'

'Not looking at you enough?' Kirsten frowned. 'What does he mean? Of course I looked at you.'

'You're not keeping eye contact with me for long enough.' Cal mimicked Theo's theatrical broken English. 'Not enough emotion, Kirsten…we need more fire.'

Not enough emotion; hell, that was a laugh, Kirsten thought derisively. Theo should have been in her kitchen this morning, or in Cal's car last night. She shied away from that thought quickly.

'He wants us to practise looking at each other.'

Kirsten slowed the car, miscalculated what she was doing and crunched through the gears.

She saw Cal grimace. 'Glad this isn't my car,' he said.

'Is that some kind of joke?'

'No. I really am glad this isn't my car. You should drive an automatic, Kirsten—'

She glared at him. 'I'm talking about us practising looking at each other; I mean, that has to be some kind of a wind-up, right?'

Cal met her eyes innocently.

'No…there's a whole list of things like that here.' He waved the sheet of paper airily in her direction and she saw a full page of what looked like stage directions.

'Theo must have been up all night writing those,' Kirsten said tersely. 'Are they all centring on my faults?'

'No…to be fair, there are a few things he wants to draw to my attention…'

'Just a few?' Kirsten watched Cal as he flicked his finger searchingly down the long…long list then turned the page.

'Here we are. He thinks when we have that argument about the working rota that I need to concentrate more on my motivation.'

'What's your motivation?'

'I want to take you to bed.'

'Pardon?' She switched her eyes from the road.

'That's what my motivation is. I want to take you to bed and—'

'Yes, OK, I get the picture.' Kirsten felt herself blush uncomfortably.

Cal flicked over another few pages. 'He has highlighted a few scenes that he thinks we need to run through. He says that unless we can work something out they are going to present a problem.'

'What kind of problem?'

Cal shut the folder. 'Quite frankly, Kirsten, reading between the lines, I think that Theo has picked up very quickly on the fact that we are not entirely…easy around each other.'

Kirsten's hands tightened on the steering wheel.

'And in a romantic picture I'm sure you'll agree that's a bit of a problem.'

'I tried to tell you that when you told me you had accepted the part,' she reminded him curtly.

'Come on, honey. We're professionals.'

'Don't call me that.'

'What, a professional?'

'Honey...don't call me honey,' she grated.

'There you go again. You're really uptight, Kirsty. You need to relax.'

That had to be the understatement of the year, Kirsten thought. But there wasn't much chance of relaxation while he was around.

Cal closed the folder. 'Do you remember our first date?' he asked her suddenly.

Kirsten didn't answer. She wanted to say no. But that was a blatant lie. She remembered it all too clearly. 'Not really,' she said dismissively. 'What's that to do with anything?'

'We went to that party from hell,' Cal continued as if she hadn't spoken.

'That wasn't our first date, it was our second; on our first date we took a picnic to the beach.' She looked over at him and caught the gleam of satisfaction in his blue eyes.

He smiled. 'So we did...' he drawled.

And she knew right then that he had set a trap and she had walked neatly inside. He remembered their first date just as clearly as she did. 'What about it anyway?' she asked crossly.

'I was just thinking that when we have difficulty acting in these love scenes...when we feel tense around each other...maybe we should try a bit of method acting. We could try and picture ourselves back on that beach three years ago. We could remember the heat of the sun on our bodies, and the even greater heat inside when we looked at each other.' Cal's voice was deep and huskily seductive, and somehow it summoned up the memories of that day in an evocative and electric way.

She glanced across at him and a shiver of pure nostalgia raced through her body from nowhere.

There was the sound of a horn furiously cutting the air. Hurriedly Kirsten returned her attention to the road.

'So what do you think of my idea?' he asked after a few moments when they were on a quieter section of the road.

'Quite frankly, as a method of relaxation I think it stinks,' she said, pulling herself together.

'So what do you suggest we do, then?'

She shrugged. 'Maybe I'll just try and picture myself with somebody else,' she said flippantly. 'That might work.'

She flicked a glance at him and saw that he wasn't too enamoured of the suggestion; there was a gleam of annoyance in his blue eyes now. She smiled to herself. It felt good to dent that massive male ego of his. The man was too damn sure of himself by far.

'So who are you planning to use as your subject; not Jason surely?' Cal grated derisively.

'Why not? I had no problem playing a love scene opposite him once before.'

'Well, good for you,' Cal muttered sarcastically. 'Is that when the love bug between you bit? When you were between the sheets on set?'

Kirsten's hands tightened on the steering wheel, but she forced herself to make no reply.

'It's no wonder you can so easily picture yourself working opposite Jason,' Cal continued, still with that edge in his voice. 'You two have done a lot of work together, haven't you? A show on Broadway and that TV special; was it by accident or design?'

'It was just by coincidence, that's all.'

'I do hope he's not going to pine away for you while you're in San Francisco.'

She threw Cal a scathing look. 'As a matter of fact, he's coming to San Francisco next week and we are going to meet up. Not that it's any of your business.'

'They say absence makes the heart grow fonder, don't they?' Cal drawled. 'Maybe he'll propose?'

Kirsten was about to snap, Don't be ridiculous, Jason

just happened to be coming to San Francisco on business next week anyway…then she stopped herself. She had been right first time. It was none of his business.

They travelled onwards in silence. Kirsten thought about Jason. She supposed if she allowed their friendship to develop it could get serious. Jason liked her…maybe he more than liked her. And she liked him…but not enough, at least not in the way you should feel about a man you wanted to be serious with. Yet she didn't want to lose Jason's friendship.

Was there something wrong with her? she wondered suddenly. Two years was a long time to go without any serious involvement. Maybe she just wasn't ready?

There had been no one since Cal. The very idea of starting a new relationship, learning to trust someone, placing herself in that vulnerable position again of falling in love and losing control…scared her deeply.

'Shall we stop and have a coffee?' Cal asked suddenly. 'There's a good hotel further down here, just off the main road.'

She glanced at the clock on the dashboard and was surprised to see that she had been driving for nearly two hours. 'Yes…OK; I want to try and ring my parents.'

'To tell them you'll be late?'

'To tell them I won't be coming.'

Whatever Cal thought about that, he kept his opinion to himself, and for that Kirsten was grateful.

The hotel Cal directed her to had a small coffee lounge just inside the main foyer. They sat amongst the potted palms and listened to the piped music and tried to pretend that they couldn't hear the women who were arguing at the other side of the room about whether or not that really was *the* Cal McCormick.

After a few moments when a waiter didn't arrive Cal got up and strolled over towards the bar to place their order.

Kirsten took the opportunity to phone her mother, glad

that Cal was out of earshot. She didn't want him listening while she tried to explain why she couldn't go home.

Her mother answered the phone almost immediately. 'We're so looking forward to seeing you, darling,' she said excitedly. 'Where are you?'

'I'm not quite sure actually.' Kirsten glanced away from where Cal stood at the bar, towards the window and noticed that the day was darkening; grey storm clouds were sweeping in from the direction of the sea. 'But I'm not making as good time as I'd hoped. The fact is, Mum, I don't think I'm going to be able to call today.'

'Oh, Kirsten! Your father is going to be so disappointed...so am I.'

Kirsten felt a pang of guilt hit her. 'How is Dad?'

'Not so good, but he brightened considerably when I told him you were coming. He came and did a bit of shopping with me this morning. We're going to put a pot roast in the oven...I thought you'd be here in an hour.'

Kirsten glanced at her watch. 'Well, I'm further than that away and—'

'Never mind.' Her mother cut across her brightly. 'We can eat later. The meat isn't in the oven yet. Come for dinner instead.'

Kirsten took a deep breath and decided to be honest. 'The thing is, Mum, that I'm in a bit of a complicated situation; I'm with Cal, you see, and—'

'Oh, Kirsten!'

Kirsten was quite unprepared for her mother's squeal of delight. 'Oh, darling, I'm so thrilled. You don't know what this means to me and your father. We read a few things in the paper about the two of you getting back together, but we didn't dare hope—'

'Mum!' Kirsten cut in quickly. 'We are just working together. I explained the situation a few weeks ago—'

'Yes...you did. And your father said at the time,

''Kirsten is still in love with him; they're going to get back together.'' But even so I wasn't sure—'

'Mum, you've got it—'

'I'm so pleased that he's there with you, Kirsty. Now I know you two have a lot of catching-up to do, and you probably want to be on your own, but if you could come for a visit today it would mean so much. It would really brighten your dad up to see Cal.'

'But you've got it wrong about Cal and me—'

'You know your dad has to go to his doctor tomorrow for the results of his latest tests—this is just what he needs to take his mind off things.' Her mother continued as if Kirsten hadn't spoken.

Kirsten weakened. She did want to see her father, and if she could help to make him feel better in any way she'd do it like a shot. But she couldn't pretend to be back with Cal...

'There's a lovely picture in this morning's paper of you and Cal arriving at a première last night,' her mother said softly into the sudden silence. 'You looked so good together—'

Kirsten saw Cal coming back towards her.

'Look, we'll come for dinner.' She cut across her mother swiftly. 'I do want to see you and Dad; I just don't want you to get the wrong idea. There is nothing going on between Cal and me, honestly, Mum. We're just working together.'

'Yes, dear, shall we expect you late afternoon?'

'OK—'

'Great, and tell Cal I'll make his favourite...apple pie.' Her mother put the phone down before she could say another word.

'Problems?' Cal asked as he sat back down and met the full blast of annoyance from her shimmering green eyes.

'Yes, actually. My parents think we are getting back to

gether, and my mother didn't seem to want to listen to me when I said we weren't.'

'Really?' Cal didn't sound in the slightest bit concerned.

'I've had to tell her we will drop by to see them. They're cooking dinner for us.'

'That's no hardship.' Cal looked pleased.

'Yeah...well, while you are there, do you think you could categorically deny these rumours that are springing up about us in the papers, before Mum starts planning her wedding outfit?'

Cal grinned. 'As bad as that, is it?'

'Worse.'

'I'll see what I can do,' Cal said. 'Meanwhile, shall we order a light lunch here?'

CHAPTER FIVE

IT WAS starting to rain as Kirsten pulled her car through her parents' front gate. Up ahead, the familiar house threw a welcoming golden light into the murkiness of the afternoon.

Kirsten's parents' lived in a dormer cottage with white clapboard sidings and a pitched grey roof that sloped out over a long porch. In the summer months they often sat on the porch, looking out towards the ocean that was so close that they had their own small shingle cove at the end of the garden.

Today, however, the misty rain obliterated the view of the sea. The clouds were so low that they couldn't even see her father's old boat that was moored a little way out on a wooden jetty.

Not even Candy, the family's golden retriever, was out on the porch. However, as soon as they stepped from the car the front door opened and Candy shot out and nearly knocked Kirsten and Cal over with the strength of her welcome.

'I think she remembers me,' Cal said as he bent to pet the dog.

'Of course she remembers you,' Kirsten's mother said, reaching to give her ex-son-in-law a kiss as he walked into the hall. 'Gosh, Cal, it's really good to see you,' she said warmly.

'It's good to see you too.' Cal straightened and beamed down at Lynn. 'You haven't changed a bit; you're as gorgeous as ever.'

'Oh, get on with you,' Lynn laughed. 'And you're as charming as ever.'

Kirsten's mother was an attractive woman. She was sixty, and her short hair was pure white, but she was still slim, with the same green eyes and striking bone-structure as Kirsten.

'Hi, Mum.' Kirsten reached to kiss her mother. She supposed Cal was right; Lynn hadn't changed in the two years since Cal had been here, but the same couldn't be said for Kirsten's father. Even in the two weeks since Kirsten had last seen him, Robert Brindle had changed.

Her father had always been a well-built man, broad and strong like Cal, but recently he had lost so much weight that he looked frail somehow, as if he was shrinking away.

'How are you, Dad?' Kirsten reached to give him a hug.

'All the better for seeing you.' Robert's eyes twinkled with merriment and for a moment he looked like his old self as he pulled away from her. 'Especially as you have brought Cal home with you.' He reached out a hand and Cal took it in a hearty handshake. 'Good to see you, son,' Robert said gruffly.

Kirsten felt her throat tighten suddenly, the warmth of her parents' greeting for Cal suddenly punching home the fact of how much they had loved him; quite simply he had been the son they'd never had. Her father especially had liked having Cal around. They had enjoyed an easy camaraderie, had talked sport and fishing. She remembered one weekend Cal had even helped him to renovate the boat, scraping the hull and painting it alongside him.

She should have followed her instincts and not brought Cal here, she thought grimly. This was stirring up memories for her parents as well as herself and it wasn't fair.

'So how are things in the land of Hollywood?' Robert asked as he led the way back through to the lounge.

'Can't complain, Robert, we're ticking along.' A roaring log fire burnt in the stone fireplace. Cal sat down in one of the chintz chairs next to it and held his hands out to the flames. 'The old homestead looks just as good as ever,' he remarked, glancing around the cosy interior. 'I see you've got Kirsten's piano.' His eyes flicked over the baby grand that sat easily in the window. 'Don't you play any more, Kirsten?'

He looked back at her and she felt her heart jump uncomfortably. The piano had been a wedding present from him and once upon a time it had sat very grandly in their own home in LA. 'There wasn't room for it in my new apartment,' she told him uncomfortably, wishing now that she had defied sentiment and got rid of it.

'Kirsten plays for us when she visits, don't you, honey?' her dad said fondly. 'It's quite a treat to listen to her; she's as brilliant a pianist as ever.'

'You're just a bit biased, Dad,' Kirsten said with a smile.

'No, your dad is right. You have a great talent. I used to love to listen to you play as well.' Cal's soft, huskily spoken words sent a *frisson* of reminiscence through her, conjuring up an image of them as a newly married couple, very much in love, cuddling each other by that piano.

Only they hadn't been very much in love, Kirsten told herself fiercely. It had all been an illusion...a sham.

'And Kirsten tells me you've still got your boat?' Cal turned his attention back to her father.

'Yes, but the *Seafarer* isn't living up to her name these days. She needs a lot of work, and I haven't got the energy for it any more.' Robert sat down opposite him. 'Maybe I will have once the weather picks up again.'

'If I could I'd come and help out with her,' Cal reflected. 'I always enjoyed working on the boat with you.'

'I know,' Robert said huskily. 'We had some good times on that boat, you and I.'

Oh, for heaven's sake Kirsten thought crossly. How could her father be so easily taken in? Maybe Cal did help with the boat in the past, but that had been in the days before he had become such a big movie star. There was no way that Cal would be interested in messing about with that old boat and getting his hands dirty now. It would be way beneath him.

Candy padded across and sat down beside him, resting her head adoringly on his knee.

Kirsten groaned inwardly. Weren't dogs supposed to be good judges of character? 'Not you too, Candy…please,' she muttered.

'Sorry, darling, did you say something?' Lynn looked over at her.

'No…just that there's a lovely smell coming from the kitchen,' Kirsten said cheerily. Then decided she had better start putting her folks straight before this situation got any worse.

'Now, Mum…Dad, I don't know what you've been reading in the papers,' she began briskly, 'but Cal and I just want to tell you that there is no truth in the rumours that we are getting back together. No truth in them whatsoever.' She glanced over at Cal pointedly. 'Isn't that right, Cal?'

Cal shrugged. 'These papers get a lot of things wrong.' He spread his hands out in appeal. 'I mean, I read in one of those articles last week that you are thirty-one, Kirsten. Now, come on, that kind of a mistake is unacceptable…isn't it? We all know you're twenty-seven.'

Kirsten saw her mother opening her mouth to tell him that the paper had been quite right, and then close it again as she thought better of the correction.

Cal looked over at Kirsten, his blue eyes glimmering with amusement.

He knew very well how old she was, Kirsten thought with annoyance. 'Never mind about my age, Cal,' she muttered. 'Will you please just tell Mum and Dad that they've got everything else wrong? We are simply working together on a movie. The words are written down for us.'

'Yes, that's right, we're back working together.' Cal smiled. Then changed the subject. 'You know, Kirsten's right—there is a lovely smell coming out of the kitchen. Have you been baking, Lynn?'

'Yes, your favourite, as I remember—home-made apple pie.' Her mother turned towards the kitchen. 'I better go and check on dinner,' she said.

Kirsten turned to follow her from the room. She was going to reinforce the fact that she and Cal weren't an item, but as she watched her mother open and close the oven door she found herself worrying about her dad instead. 'I know you said Dad was a bit brighter. But he looks as if he's lost more weight.'

'His appetite hasn't been good. But I think it's just the stress of not being well. You know how active he's always been. He hates having to take things easy…feels frustrated that he can't do things around the house, can't even potter about on his boat. He hasn't been an easy patient.'

'I can imagine.' Kirsten nodded. 'If I wasn't tied up with this film I'd come and help—'

'I'm managing fine, Kirsten. The doctor says that as long as he keeps taking his medication, and continues to take it easy, he will be OK.' The smell of cinnamon and apple filled the warmth of the room as Lynn put two apple pies on trays to cool. 'You bringing Cal here today has helped him tremendously. It's a real tonic for him; I haven't seen him as bright and as happy as this in a long while now.'

Kirsten frowned. 'But I don't want him to get the wrong idea. Like I said in the lounge, there's nothing between Cal and me now—'

'We'll see.' Her mother smiled.

'Cal and I don't even like each other any more.'

'Yes, dear.' Her mother turned to take some potatoes from the top of the stove. 'Do you think I should pour some of my home-made lemonade or would Cal prefer a beer?'

'Mum—'

'He used to like my home-made lemonade, didn't he?'

Kirsten stared at her mother's back in utter frustration. Why couldn't she just accept what she was telling her?

'Cal's changed, Mum. He's not the same person any more. He's not the man I married. We could never get back together again because we have nothing in common now—'

'I haven't changed that much.' Cal's droll voice from the kitchen doorway made them both jump. 'I still have the same likes and dislikes and I'm sure I'd still like your mother's home-made lemonade.'

Kirsten's heart thumped angrily as she watched her mother smile warmly at him. What the hell was Cal playing at? He was supposed to be backing her up!

'I still keep the lemonade out in the garage. Would you do the honours, Cal, and fetch in a bottle?' her mother asked happily.

'Certainly.'

Kirsten watched Cal disappear out of the back door and then after a moment's hesitation she followed him.

The rain beat mistily against her skin, blurring her vision as she ran across the wet grass after him.

'Who said the sun always shines in southern California?' Cal asked with a grin as she followed him into the darkness of the garage.

Kirsten ignored him. 'You just have to be Mr Popular,' she said angrily, 'don't you?'

'What are you talking about, Kirsten?' He switched on the overhead light and moved away from her past her father's car to the storage area at the back of the large garage.

'You know what I'm talking about...I want you to tell my parents that it's all over between us...that we have no interest left in each other.'

'Yeah...well, that's not so easy, is it?' he said.

'No. Because you are so damned tied up with your own image of being Mr Perfect. So instead you make me out to be the big baddie. Oh, Kirsten's the unreasonable one…Kirsten's the one who wanted the divorce. But that's not true, is it, Cal? Why can't you just tell them the truth?'

'I never told your parents that you wanted the divorce. They know what happened. The truth is that neither of us could cope with losing Bethany.'

'I don't want to talk about that.' The words trembled on her lips.

'And even now after all this time you can't open up to me…you can't admit the truth.' His eyes narrowed on her. 'Kirsten, I wasn't there for you when you needed me and for that I'm truly sorry.' He said the words huskily. 'But I was grieving as well, you know.'

She shook her head, her eyes wide with disbelief. 'Maybe you were sad for a while,' she muttered. 'But let's face it, Cal…what happened…left you free to pursue your career and—'

'How dare you say that?' he grated angrily. 'What happened was that I lost my child. You can't even bring yourself to say her name, can you? We called her Bethany…we had her baptised at the hospital, Kirsten, remember? We christened her Bethany Jane McCormick.'

'I don't want to have this conversation with you.' Her voice caught on a sob of panic. 'I only want you to do as I ask.' He reached out to catch hold of her arm as she tried to swing away from him and the movement caused some dustsheets to fall beside them.

Both of them stilled as they saw the baby's crib and the bundle of soft toys. The crib was still in new condition with the plastic wrapping on the covers.

Kirsten remembered her mother telling them she'd bought a crib for the baby. 'I'm keeping it out in the garage,' she had told them cheerfully. 'Just for another few weeks until you bring the baby home. That way we're not tempting fate and inviting bad luck.'

The memory ran like a shiver down her spine. She tore her eyes away from the crib and desperately tried to tur

her mind away from the past and concentrate on their conversation. 'So just back me up, Cal, and make...make
things clear to my parents. They like you and it's not fair
to raise their hopes and offer them false expectations.'

'Imagine them keeping that crib all this time,' Cal said
instead, his eyes locked on the shelves beside them.

Kirsten didn't follow his gaze. 'I...I keep telling them
they need to have a clear-out.' Her voice trembled slightly.
'It's the same up in the house; the cupboards are full of
old stuff from way back.'

'Yes, but this is stuff they bought for Bethany.' Cal
turned and picked up one of the teddy bears. He stood
looking down at it, and for a moment he looked lost. He
rubbed a thumb almost tenderly over the golden fur.

Watching him, Kirsten felt as if a hand had gripped hold
of her heart and was squeezing it with all its might.

'We had such high hopes for the future, didn't we,
Kirsten?' he murmured huskily. 'And then somewhere
along the way it all went wrong.'

'Maybe it was just never meant to be in the first place.'
Her voice was low and almost drummed out by the sound
of rain on the flat roof.

'Do you really believe that?' He turned and looked at
her then, noting the shadows in the beauty of her green
eyes and the extreme pallor of her fair skin.

'I don't know.' She looked away helplessly. 'I don't
know what I believe any more.' She shivered suddenly in
the cool air.

He put the toy down. 'If I could turn the clock back and
make everything right I would do it, Kirsten,' he said softly.
'If I could have saved Bethany...'

In those few moments she heard his grief, felt it like a
razor-sharp image of her own. It stopped her in her tracks,
made her look at him as if she had never seen him before.
He looked...sounded so vulnerable. Cal, vulnerable? It was
hard to believe. But it was there clearly in his face, in his

tone. He looked completely shattered and it was real emotion. Suddenly she felt protective of him. Wanted to hold him, comfort him. How could she have been so blind as not to see how Bethany's death had affected him, just as it had devastated her?

The realisation shocked her to her core and guilt thrust through her from out of nowhere. She had been so wrong to accuse him of blithely putting the loss of their child behind him without difficulty, so…terribly…appallingly wrong.

'You couldn't have done anything to save Bethany…Cal No one could,' she whispered unsteadily.

He reached out and touched his thumb against the coolness of her cheek, much in the same way he had with the toy a few moments ago. It was just a gentle caress but the shock of it reverberated all the way through her body.

She looked up at him wordlessly and met the warmth of his eyes. For a while neither of them spoke, and the emotion that flared between them was hard to understand Kirsten felt herself holding her breath as tension spiralled inside her like a clock spring being overwound.

Then suddenly she found herself folded into his arms and held tightly. The sound of his heartbeats merged with the racing of hers and the rhythmic drumming of the rain on the roof.

She wanted to tell him she was sorry, that she understood what he'd gone through now, but her throat was closed with the weight of her emotions and she didn't dare try to speak for fear she would cry.

Then she pulled away from him, trying desperately to gather her senses together.

'Kirsten…' he called after her as she turned blindly for the door. She didn't look back…didn't dare stay a moment longer in that room.

Her heart was still racing unevenly as she entered the warmth of the kitchen again.

'Did you find the lemonade?' Her mother glanced around at her.

She shook her head. 'You need to clear that garage out, Mum.' Her voice trembled alarmingly.

'I know…' Her mother looked concerned suddenly. 'Are you OK, honey?'

She nodded. But she didn't feel OK.

Cal followed her in through the back door a few moments later.

'I think the weather is getting worse out there,' he said as Lynn looked over at him questioningly.

'At least you found the lemonade,' she said.

'Yes, hidden away right at the back.' He put down two bottles on the counter.

He sounded at ease, as if the scene between them outside hadn't happened. Kirsten couldn't bring herself to look at him; she kept remembering the pain in his voice a few moments ago, and the warmth of his arms around her.

'Shall I carve that joint for you, Lynn?' Cal asked, noting it sitting next to the oven.

'That would be great.' Lynn slanted a look over at her daughter. 'Why don't you go and keep your dad company while I dish up dinner?'

Kirsten didn't argue with that; she was just glad of the excuse to vacate the room.

Her father wasn't in the lounge and Kirsten sat by the piano in the front window, idly flicking her fingers over the keys as she waited for him.

How could she have been so wrong to think that Cal had dealt with the death of their child easily? The gnawing pain of guilt lay heavily upon her. How had she missed the fact that he was suffering Bethany's loss with equal pain?

Kirsten didn't often allow herself to think about those dark days, but now she forced herself to look back, searching desperately for something, some clue to what she had missed.

She had cried so much after Bethany died that she had been surprised that there were any more tears left in her body to fall...but Cal...Cal had been so strong; in fact, there had been no great display of any emotion from him whatsoever, now that she thought about it.

At the time she had told herself he was able to maintain that steely front because he didn't feel Bethany's loss as acutely as she did. After all, he hadn't carried her for nine months...he hadn't even been there when she had died.

She frowned; remembering those judgements now with a sickening churning sensation inside.

Cal had asked her once if she blamed him for not being there. She had told him that she didn't...and it was true...

How could she blame him for not being there? she asked herself reasonably. It wasn't his fault, she knew that. Even if he'd been there he wouldn't have been able to do anything. It was one of those cruel flukes of nature...the birth cord tangling around the baby...

She had been two weeks overdue and she hadn't been feeling well that day. Cal had had a meeting booked for that evening and he had wanted to cancel it, but she had told him not to. She remembered being quite firm about it. 'I'll be fine,' she had told him resolutely. 'There's absolutely no point you staying here with me. I'm going to relax, listen to some music. I'll phone you if I need you.'

He'd been gone for less than an hour when the pains had started. She hadn't panicked; she'd rung the studio and left a message for him, then caught a cab to the hospital.

But by the time Cal had reached her bedside it had been too late.

She allowed herself to think about that moment when he had come into her room in the hospital, the look in his eyes and the terrible...terrible anguish of what had happened. He had sat down next to her and reached out for her, but she had turned away.

Her heart froze as she remembered herself doing that.

Her fingers slipped on the keys of the piano, sending a discordant note jarring through the silence.

Guilt licked a heated course through her body. She'd judged Cal harshly. Just because he hadn't broken down it didn't mean he hadn't felt the same pain, suffered as much as she had when their child died.

She had been so wrong.

But Cal was equally wrong to say that their marriage had failed because they had both been unable to cope with Bethany's death...that wasn't true, she told herself angrily.

The marriage had failed because he had deceived her; he had married her knowing that he loved somebody else. It had been nothing to do...with the baby.

'You OK, sweetheart?' Her father came into the room and put a hand on her shoulder.

'Yes...' She couldn't look up at him.

'Why don't you play something on the piano? It seems ages since you've sat there.'

Kirsten instinctively ran her fingers over the keys, playing an old favourite of his.

It was typical that Cal should want to shift the blame for their marriage break-up away from him and Maeve. But he couldn't rewrite history like that. Her marriage had fallen apart because Cal hadn't loved her.

The final blow had been when she had caught Cal and Maeve Ryan in each other's arms.

It had only been a couple of months after she had lost Bethany. Despite Cal's protests, she had been submerging herself in work, it had been preferable to skirting around each other on the rare occasions they were alone in the house together. Kirsten had needed something else to think about, something to focus on. But on this particular day she had arrived back early from the studio.

She could still picture the scene in the lounge, Cal's arms tightly around the other woman as he held her close. 'You know I want to be with you in London, Maeve...' His voice was deep and husky with emotion, an emotion that seared into Kirsten like a hot iron. 'But Kirsten needs me right now and I've got to be here for her.'

'I know...poor Kirsten, I feel so sorry for her.'

The sympathy in the woman's voice literally turned Kirsten's stomach. She didn't want her sympathy, nor did she want Cal's charity. That he was staying with her because he felt sorry for her was unbearable to her.

'I'll try and come over to England later—'

Kirsten backed away from the whispered promises. She left the house and spent hours driving aimlessly around, wondering what she should do.

No clear answer came to her until she returned home. Cal was alone, looking out of the front windows as she pulled up.

'Where have you been?' he asked anxiously. 'I phoned the studio and they said you'd left hours ago.'

'I needed to be on my own for a while.'

'I've decided not to take that job in London,' he said calmly as she walked to the sideboard to pour herself a drink.

'Don't bother sacrificing yourself on my account; I want you to go,' she said firmly. The words came as a surprise to her; she hadn't planned at all to say them, in fact, she hadn't realised that she had the strength to say them. 'The sooner you go the better. Our marriage is over.'

Once the words started she felt stronger...almost empowered. It was as if she was taking back the control of her life, and surprisingly it helped bring back some feeling somewhere into her body, even if that feeling was nothing more than anger.

'You still play as beautifully as ever.' Her father leaned closer and she tried to smile up at him, but she knew her eyes glistened, over-bright with emotion.

'What's really happening between you and Cal?' her da

asked gently. 'And don't give me all this garbage that you are just working together.'

'We *are* just working together.' Kirsten stopped playing and in the silence she could hear her heart beating in time to its own music.

'Come on, Kirsty. You may be a grown woman but you're still my little girl.' Her dad smiled at her. 'I've always known when you weren't telling me the whole truth.'

'But I am—'

Robert shook his head. 'Do you know what I think? I think you're lying to yourself and that you're still in love with him.'

'No, I'm not!' Her voice was a strangled whisper. 'Really, I'm not.'

'A second chance for happiness doesn't come along very often in life, Kirsten. Take some advice from an old man and think very carefully before you throw it away. Or you might regret it for the rest of your life.'

'You're way off track, Dad,' Kirsten reiterated. 'We don't feel that way about each other any more. We've moved on.'

'If I'm wrong I'm sorry, but I'd like to see you happy again, Kirsten, before…well, before too long, and Cal's a good man. Give the matter your deepest thought.'

CHAPTER SIX

'ANOTHER glass of lemonade, Kirsten?' Cal asked her when there was a lull in the conversation around the dinner table.

'No, thank you.' She avoided meeting his eyes across the candlelit table.

Her father claimed Cal's attention once more. They were having a lively conversation about football. 'So what do you think the outcome will be?' Robert asked jovially.

'I think they'll win,' Cal said as he topped up Robert's glass. 'They played so well in their last game that they are looking invincible at the moment.'

Kirsten tried to tune out from Cal's conversation with her father as her mother asked her where she would be staying in San Francisco.

'The studio have arranged an apartment for me. I'll write the address down for you before I go. But you can always reach me on my mobile.'

'How long do you think you'll be there?'

Kirsten was just about to reply when she heard Cal say, 'If you like, Robert, I can get tickets for the game. We could go see it together.'

'Really! Cal, those tickets are like gold dust,' her father said in some excitement. 'How can you manage that?'

Kirsten's head jerked up then and she looked across at Cal.

'Well, there's no point being famous if you can't pull a few strings now and then.' Cal smiled at Kirsten as he met her eyes. 'Isn't that right, Kirsty?'

'Not being that famous, I wouldn't know,' she said succinctly. What the hell was Cal playing at? she wondered He was openly and deliberately flouting her request. Instead of emphasising the fact that he wasn't part of their lives any more, he seemed to be going the other way. Suggesting a trip to the football game with her father was definitely an encroachment back into her family.

'I don't think you'll be able to go to that game anyway, Cal,' she told him pointedly.

'No? Why not?' He seemed totally unaware of what he had done. Even as he met her eyes across the table, his expression was one of blank innocence.

'Well, for one thing, we don't know what free time we're going to get over the next few months. You know what it's like when we're filming.' Her eyes narrowed on him in silent warning, willing him to take the hint. After the way her father had been speaking to her earlier she felt it was now imperative for Cal to make his position clear, tell them he wasn't interested in getting back together with her.

'True. But I'll have a word with Theo…a lot of the crew are probably going to the game as well.'

'It would be great if you could,' her father said enthusiastically.

'Leave it with me, Robert.' Cal smiled.

He knew exactly what he was doing, Kirsten realised as she glared at him across the table. He was playing at being Mr Popular again.

'More apple pie, anyone?' Lynn cut across the tension.

'Actually, Mum, I think we should go.' Kirsten glanced at her watch. 'We've still got a few hours' drive ahead of us.'

'Why don't you stay the night?' Lynn asked. 'You can set off first thing tomorrow. You haven't got to report in until the day after, and we see so little of you these days.'

Kirsten hesitated; she knew how much it would mean to her parents. 'Thanks, Mum, but we really can't, we've got to find our accommodation tonight and it will take a day to settle in and go over some work before filming starts early Tuesday. Besides, you've only got one spare bedroom, where do you intend to put Cal...in the garage?' She tried to sound jovially unconcerned about where Cal went, whilst at the same time pushing home her point that he wouldn't be welcome in her room.

'There's a pull-out settee in your room, Kirsten,' her mother continued, undeterred. 'You used to be married, after all, so I'm sure you could double up in there for one night.'

'Mother!' Kirsten stared at her mother in absolute horror.

'I don't think this is for my ears,' Robert said with a wry grin. He pushed his chair back from the table. 'Excuse me, I've got to get my tablets.'

'Don't look at me like that, Kirsten.' Her mother shook her head in admonishment as Robert left the room. 'You could share the room with Cal. It's no big deal; you're both sensible adults. I don't know why you're making such a fuss.' She got up from the table. 'I'll put the kettle on and we'll have a coffee while you think about it.'

'I don't need to think about it,' Kirsten said somewhat wildly. Had her mother gone mad? She'd rather share her room with Dracula than Cal McCormick.

Cal met her gaze across the table. There was a glint of humour in his blue eyes that irritated her further. 'What's the matter?' he asked her quietly. 'Couldn't you trust yourself to be alone in a room with me?'

Her eyes narrowed on him. 'No, I might do something really stupid,' she murmured. 'Like mistake you for the dartboard or something.'

'Really?' Cal grinned. 'I like bedtime games.'

She slanted him a warning look.

'So what do you think, Cal?' Her mother brought over a pot of coffee and set it down on the table. 'The roads around here can be treacherous when this mist comes down.'

'I know, Lynn, but Kirsten's right; we really should be going.' Cal shook his head regretfully.

Her mother looked upset. 'Well, if you must.' She sighed. 'I suppose it's selfish of me to want to keep you here. It's just…I miss you both so much.'

'Oh, Mum!' Kirsten got up and gave her mother a hug. 'It will be OK. I'll come back as soon as I get a break from work.'

Lynn nodded, then pulled herself together. 'I'll just go and see how your dad is faring with his tablets. If I don't watch him, he'll be taking my multi-vitamins by mistake.'

She bustled out of the room, the swing door slamming shut behind her. Kirsten glanced over at Cal. 'Those damn journalists and the PR people at the studio have a lot to answer for,' she said in exasperation. 'That stuff in the paper has really upset her and Dad.'

'She's not upset about that, Kirsten.' Cal got up from the table and started to clear the dishes away. 'She's just going through a difficult time at the moment with your dad being ill.'

Kirsten looked over uncertainly at him.

'Look on the bright side,' Cal continued. 'Reading that stuff in the papers has probably cheered them both up.'

'But those articles are not true.'

He shrugged. 'Does that matter too much if it's helping them through a difficult time?'

'Of course it matters.' Kirsten closed the door of the dishwasher and turned it on as Cal started to rinse through the crystal glasses. 'You've got to be realistic.'

'I don't like too much realism,' Cal said with a smile. 'That's why I enjoyed that TV show you were in not long ago.'

'You watched that?' Kirsten looked over at him in astonishment.

'Yes, it was on English TV and I videotaped it. I was curious to see what kind of actress you were.'

'What did you think of the show?'

'It confirmed what the critics said about you when you were on Broadway. You've got great talent.'

'Thanks.' It was crazy how much pleasure his acknowledgement gave her.

He smiled, then said teasingly, 'Although I have to say a couple of scenes could have been improved.'

'Which ones?' She frowned.

'The love scenes didn't do you justice. As I recall, you are even more sensually alluring than the director gave you credit for. But perhaps my memory is deceiving me.'

Something about the way he said that, the husky, sexy undertones in his voice made Kirsten's heart miss a beat.

Of course, he was just teasing her. Cal was a master at flirtatious repartee; she supposed it was part of his job. She'd seen him in action many times. He could slay a woman with just one sentence and a carefully raised eyebrow.

She fell silent, drying the glasses methodically as she tried not to think too deeply about Cal or his motivations.

It seemed strange working next to him in her mother's kitchen... Almost like old times.

The last time they had done this had been their final Christmas together. A vivid memory flashed into her mind. She had been heavily pregnant that Christmas and the future had still seemed so full of promise.

She remembered Cal teasing her about the size of her stomach, telling her that there wasn't room for her in the small kitchen, that what she really needed was an aircraft hangar.

She'd splashed him with some water from the sink and he'd caught hold of her and laughingly pulled her against his chest. 'But I still love you,' he had whispered huskily against her ear. 'In fact, I'm starting to think that big is very sexy.'

Was that the last time Cal had told her he loved her? she

wondered. And felt the cold, raw ache of pain hit her deep
inside.

Cal handed her the last of the crystal glasses that he was
rinsing under the tap and her eyes connected with his for
just a moment.

Was he remembering the last time they had stood here?

The phone rang in the other room and she could hear her
mother chatting to someone.

There was silence between them as they continued to
work.

'Are you OK? You're very quiet,' Cal asked.

'Of course I'm OK.' She answered him brightly, possibly
too brightly.

'Good.' He watched as she put the glasses away in the
cupboard. 'Listen, about what happened between us outside—'

The memory of them holding tightly to each other rushed
back with all its force and with all its weight of emotion,
hitting into her again like a speeding car out of control.

'I think we should move on, Cal,' she cut across him
quietly.

'There are still things we need to talk about, Kirsten,
issues that need resolving.' His voice was hesitant.

'What's the point?' She forced herself to look over at
him then and meet his steady, clear gaze.

A look of annoyance passed over the handsome features.
'I think there is a point. For a start, we've got to work
together, Kirsty. How the hell are we going to put across
a reputable performance as lovers if we can't even be
friends?'

She might have known that Cal's priority was work.
They wouldn't even be standing here together now if it
weren't for that. He probably wouldn't even have kissed
her the other night if it weren't for that.

Before she could make any reply she could hear her
mother calling them from the other room, an urgent note

in her voice. Immediately they both hurried out to see what was wrong.

Her father was sitting in his chair by the fire and he looked ashen; her mother was leaning over him, asking if she should phone for a doctor.

'No, I'll be all right in a minute.' Robert tried to smile up at his daughter as she went to his side. 'Sorry about this, sweetheart, but it's nothing to worry about.'

Kirsten didn't believe him for a second; he looked so frail that she felt fear welling up inside her.

'Shall we phone a doctor, Robert?' Cal asked, his voice soothing and calm.

'No...no, I'll just take another tablet.' Robert looked at his wife. 'Will you get them from beside my bed?'

Lynn hurried off to do as he asked and Kirsten sat on the arm of her father's chair and put her arm around him, drawing him close against her. 'You'll be OK, Dad,' she said softly, trying to reassure herself as much as him. 'You'll be OK.'

'Yes...listen, Kirsten, will you do something for me?' he asked suddenly...urgently.

'Anything.'

'Will you and Cal stay tonight? I'll be fine but I think your mother would appreciate it if you were here...just for a bit of moral support. I have to go for the result of my tests tomorrow morning, and your mother will be worried about it now, especially as I've just taken a bad turn. You staying the night will take her mind off it and make all the difference.'

'Yes, of course we'll stay,' Kirsten said instantly. She didn't want to leave him now anyway. She looked over at Cal. 'You don't mind, do you?'

'No. Not at all,' Cal said firmly.

'Thank you.' Her father reached out and squeezed her hand. His grip was surprisingly firm, considering he was so weak.

'Great news,' Robert said cheerily as Lynn came back into the room with his tablets and a glass of water. 'Kirsten and Cal have agreed to stay the night.'

'Have they?' Startled, Lynn looked over at her daughter and smiled tremulously. 'Thank you.'

'You don't need to thank me…' Kirsten frowned slightly as her father pulled away from her and reached for the remote control of the TV. 'My programme is on in a minute,' he explained with a smile.

Kirsten met Cal's eyes across the room. 'I'll go out to the car and bring the cases in,' he said, 'if you give me the keys.'

Kirsten got up and went into the kitchen to get her bag. She looked around as Cal followed her into the room. 'Do you think Dad is OK?' she asked him anxiously. 'Maybe we should have insisted on calling a doctor.'

Cal hesitated. 'We'll keep an eye on him and see how he is later in the evening. He seems all right again now…maybe it was just a panic attack.'

'Maybe.' Kirsten nodded. 'He did seem to brighten up very quickly when I said we'd stay.'

'Yeah, he did, didn't he?'

Their eyes met and she knew that he was wondering the same thing she was—had her father just staged that little performance so that they would stay?

She didn't voice the thought in case she was wrong… Her father was obviously not well anyway, and if having them around made him feel better it was probably best to go along with it.

She handed Cal her car keys. 'I'm sorry about this. You don't mind staying, do you?' she asked tentatively…realising that not so long ago he had agreed with her that they should leave.

'No. Just as long as you don't use me as a dartboard.'

She smiled shakily at him, remembering how determined

she had been not to stay tonight. 'It's amazing how a sharp shock can help jolt your priorities back into order, isn't it?'

Their hands touched as he took the keys from her. His skin felt warm against the coolness of hers. Their eyes locked in a moment of communication, then she moved away from him.

After Kirsten had checked again that her father did look brighter she went back into the kitchen to make a fresh pot of coffee.

She thought about her small bedroom upstairs. Once the pull-out settee was down it was more or less next to her double bed and there wasn't a lot of room to walk around it. How the hell was she going to get through the night, sharing that confined space with Cal?

Her hand shook as she poured the coffee and it spilt on the work surface.

She heard the front door open and close as Cal came in with the luggage.

He probably didn't want to stay in that room with her any more than she did. In fact, he was probably cursing his luck. Being stuck in a bedroom with his ex-wife for the night was hardly something to cheer about. Maybe he would prefer to sleep downstairs?

She carried the tray of coffee back through to the lounge. 'You know, I was just thinking,' she said. 'Maybe Cal could sleep down here on the settee.'

'Kirsten.' Her mother glared at her. 'It's a two-seater settee; you can't expect Cal to sleep down here when there's a perfectly good bed upstairs where he can stretch out. He's a big man.'

'OK, I'll sleep down here,' Kirsten said quietly.

'Well, you'll be sleeping with the dog,' Lynn muttered. 'And you're too tall for the settee as well.'

Cal came back into the room. 'Talk some sense into Kirsten,' her mother asked him immediately. 'She wants to sleep down here.'

Cal looked over at her and shrugged. 'I think I would be the last person Kirsten would ever listen to.'

Kirsten sipped her coffee, aware that a deafening silence had descended on the room. 'I don't mind sleeping on the settee. I'll be fine; I'll just use a blanket and it will be nice being next to the fire.'

She looked over at Cal and wondered if he'd say, Don't worry, I'll sleep down here, but he didn't. He just shrugged. 'If you want to be a martyr it's OK with me.'

She tried not to glare at him and forced herself to smile. 'Yes, fine.' Called himself a gentleman? she thought furiously. He was no gentleman, he was a total…total… Words failed her.

Her father leaned forward in his chair suddenly, his eyes alight with excitement. 'You're on TV,' he said, pointing to the box. 'It's that attractive Sandy Peterson from *Hot News*. You'll be on in a minute—she just announced it.'

Kirsten gulped the last of her coffee down. Watching that interview on TV was the last thing she needed. Out of the corner of her eye she saw Candy sitting patiently by the door. Seizing thankfully on the excuse, she got up. 'Excuse me, I'll just see to the dog.'

Candy raced out into the darkness as soon as she opened the front door. It was cool outside and there was a slight breeze now coming off the sea, but thankfully the rain and the mist had gone.

On impulse Kirsten stepped outside for some fresh air.

Candy barked at her delightedly and raced over towards the shore, glad of the company. 'You're a crazy dog,' Kirsten told her affectionately as the animal ran backwards and forwards like a mini-whirlwind of energy, jumping up at Kirsten and then racing off again. Kirsten wondered if her father hadn't been walking with her as much as he used to.

She took a deep, shuddering breath as she thought about her father's words earlier. 'I'd like to see you happy again,

Kirsten, before…well, before too long, and Cal's a good man.'

Had her father been going to say, before it's too late? Or, worse, before I go? How bad was his health? Fear struck into her like a metal fist. She knew nobody could live for ever but her father was only seventy-five; that was young nowadays, wasn't it?

She heard Cal's voice calling to her and turned to see him walking down the path towards her.

'You'll catch cold out here; it's not very warm tonight,' he said, holding out a jacket for her that she recognised as her mother's.

'I'm fine, I've taken my Echinacea.' She smiled, aware that she wasn't altogether annoyed that he'd followed her.

'What the hell is that?'

'Herbal stuff to boost your immune system.'

Cal grinned. 'You are getting more Californian by the day.'

'It really works,' Kirsten said, but she allowed him to help her on with the jacket, trying to ignore the touch of his fingers as they brushed against her skin.

'I only followed you to tell you it's safe to come back inside now,' he said with a grin. 'The interview is over.'

'Good. But I wanted to stretch my legs for a minute anyway.'

'Before you cramp them up on the settee?'

'Something like that.'

He smiled. 'Do you mind if I join you? I could do with some fresh air myself.'

'No…' She hesitated before adding truthfully, 'Actually, I'd like the company.'

'Worried about your dad, aren't you?' Cal asked gently as he fell into step beside her.

'Yes…I suppose I am.'

They followed the path down to the shore. It was a tranquil place; the only sound came from the waves against the shingle and the croak of the frogs in the long grass beside them.

'Why didn't you tell me that he's had a heart attack?' Cal asked her suddenly.

'I thought I did tell you.'

'No. You just said he wasn't well and he was having tests.'

'Well, we didn't know he'd had a heart attack until he got the results of his first tests.' Kirsten stared down at her hands. 'I don't know why you should assume that I have to tell you everything anyway,' she muttered. 'You're no longer part of the family.'

'I kind of hoped we might call a truce on that one, Kirsten,' Cal said gently. 'Even if it's only for your parents' sakes.'

He was right. Kirsten bit down on her lip, feeling suddenly selfish. If it made her father feel better to see her and Cal together, maybe she shouldn't fight it, maybe she should just go along with it for the time being. But that meant getting rid of this anger she felt for Cal and the trouble was, if she stopped being angry with him, what emotion would creep in and take its place? she wondered suddenly.

They reached the shore and stood looking out over the ocean. The sky had cleared and a full moon hung majestically in the darkness of the sky like a huge Chinese lantern; it illuminated her father's boat and sparkled over the waves crashing in on the shore, making them appear milky white against the darkness of the sand.

Candy ran up to them and barked, so Cal threw a stick for her down the beach.

'What do you really think about Dad's health?' she asked Cal suddenly.

'I'm not a doctor, Kirsten, but, from what your dad has told me, I think he'll be fine. He's just had a warning, that's all, and he says he's going to heed it.'

'Do you think so?' She turned wide eyes on him and he nodded.

'Yeah…I do. Your dad is made of tough stuff.'

It was strange how Cal could still reassure her; just the tone of his voice, the strength that emanated from him, were enough to make her feel better. In a crisis she would trust him to the ends of the earth.

But she had mistaken that strength once… That was why she hadn't recognised his grief, she realised suddenly. She had thought it meant he didn't need her. And, because she had thought he didn't need her, she hadn't been able to turn to him…had shut him out. It was strange how she could see that so clearly now; it was as if someone had shone a spotlight on her, illuminating her mistakes.

'I've really enjoyed seeing your folks again,' Cal said quietly as they watched the dog race away from them down the beach.

'The feeling was obviously mutual,' she told him sincerely.

He'd always liked it here, she remembered, had always said to her, 'You're so lucky to have your parents; don't ever take them for granted.' She supposed he felt like that because his own parents had died in a car crash when he was fourteen and he'd been sent to live with his aunt in England, where he had finished his education.

'What was it like being back in England?' she asked him tentatively now.

'It was OK. Obviously it's changed a lot since I lived there. London's still a great city, though, and Oxford University hasn't changed at all.'

'Did you see your Auntie May?'

'Yes, I saw her a few times. She's keeping well; still hasn't quite forgiven me for marrying you so quickly that she wasn't able to come to the wedding.'

'Maybe under the circumstances it's just as well that she didn't waste her time,' she murmured.

'I promised her I'd make it up to her next time I tie the knot, that I'd buy her a fabulous outfit and a wide-brimmed hat from Rodeo Drive.'

The quietly spoken words gave Kirsten a very strange feeling inside, as if all her emotions had suddenly twisted into tight knots. 'Are you planning to get married again, then?'

'Not yet.' Cal smiled at her. 'But I'm thirty-eight, Kirsten; I'm thinking maybe it would be nice to try again one day, to settle down and raise a family.'

The waves seemed to crash with even more violent force against the shore, mimicking the beat of her heart.

Candy came back with the stick and dropped it at Cal's feet, barking for him to throw it again, which he did. It was a longer throw this time and the dog went hurtling away into the darkness.

'What about you, Kirsten?' Cal asked. 'Have you any plans in that direction?'

Kirsten shook her head. She felt a bit like Candy, who was running around in the darkness now, searching in vain for the piece of driftwood. She was thirty-one. Time was moving on and maybe she should be thinking about the future. But the truth was she didn't know if she was brave enough to try again. 'I don't know,' she murmured. 'I really don't know, Cal.'

'So things aren't that serious between you and Jason then?'

'I didn't say that.' She stuck her hands in her mother's coat and tried not to shiver as the wind seemed to pull sharply around her. 'Jason's a nice guy.' Why did she feel the need to keep up this pretence about Jason? She glanced at Cal; there was a part of her that wanted to drop the barriers, tell him honestly that Jason wasn't even a con-tender when it came to thinking about marriage. But she was too scared to do that.

Cal watched her silently without saying anything. She

felt vulnerable suddenly, her face naked of make-up and accentuated by the light of the moon. What was he thinking when he was looking at her so intently?

'Why are you looking at me like that?' she asked nervously.

'I like looking at you.' He smiled. 'You've got a very arresting face.'

'Is this something to do with Theo telling us we have to practise looking at each other?' She was glad of the opportunity to lighten the atmosphere between them.

'I think Theo was more concerned about your difficulty on that score than mine.' He smiled.

'You being so damned perfect in every way?'

He grinned. 'If you say so, but I thought it was because I've never had any problem looking into your eyes.'

'Looking into any woman's eyes, for that matter.' Kirsten turned away from him and called to Candy as she ran further away from them towards the rocks.

'Did you ever miss me?' Cal asked her suddenly.

'Sorry?' She looked around at him, pretending she hadn't heard, trying to play for time. What kind of a question was that?

'Since we split up and I went to England, have you ever had a day or a moment when you missed me?'

She hesitated. The truth was she had missed him a lot. At first she had put it down to the fact that she was still living in the house they had shared, a house full of memories. There had been days when she had been desperate to talk to him, to ask him things. Nights when she had come home to an empty house and had made two drinks…before suddenly remembering that he wasn't there any more and a black weight of depression had hit. She had run through a whole gamut of emotions all the way from wanting to ask his opinion about a problem at work to why had their baby died…why had this happened to them?

When she had moved to New York for those few months

she had thought the change of scene would make her forget him. But it hadn't helped. Sometimes she had missed him so badly she had lain in bed and ached for him. But she wouldn't tell him that. She was over all that anyway.

She pretended to think about it, however, conscious of the soft hissing sound the waves were making on the sand as the tide washed out.

'No…I don't think so.' She smiled airily at him. 'Sorry if that upsets your ego.'

Cal shrugged. 'I missed you,' he said softly.

'I don't think so, Cal,' she said shakily. 'I think if there was a moment when you missed me then it was only the idea that you missed.'

'The idea?' His eyebrows rose slightly mockingly.

'Yes, the idea of having a wife…'

He frowned.

'What's the script with Maeve these days?' she asked him suddenly. 'Is she still with Brian?'

Cal hesitated fractionally. 'Yes…things are just the same.'

She swallowed hard. 'I think maybe it's time we got back to the house. I'm cold.'

Candy bounded up to them. She'd found a different piece of driftwood and it was so big this time that she could hardly carry it.

Kirsten smiled as she saw her. 'Silly dog, we can't throw that; it's too heavy.'

Candy dropped it and barked at Cal, willing him to do the honours.

'Sorry, Candy, time to go back inside,' Kirsten said, and reached to pat her.

She jumped up; her paws were wet and her tail swished backwards and forwards, shaking salt water over them. 'Ugh…Candy, stop!' Kirsten backed away from her straight into Cal and he put a steadying arm around her. For a moment she was held close against him, his hand resting against her waist. The impact, although gentle, seemed to knock the breath straight out of her and instantly she felt the flare of desire…the need to move closer.

It took all her strength to pull away. 'Sorry,' she mumbled, looking away from him.

'Candy, come on.' She busied herself calling the dog, and then they turned for the path that led back to the house in silence.

CHAPTER SEVEN

'YOU missed your interview,' her father said, reaching to switch off the TV as they came back into the room.

'Well, I know what happens, Dad,' Kirsten said with a smile, 'and it's a load of Hollywood twaddle.'

'You looked beautiful,' her mother said dreamily. 'That dress was stunning.'

'Yes, she did look beautiful, didn't she?' Cal agreed from behind her.

'I think I'll go and have a shower, put my night things on, before my head swells too much,' Kirsten said mockingly.

'I'm going to turn in as well,' her father said, getting up from his chair.

'Yes, me too.' Lynn also got to her feet and started to tidy things up. 'Would you like anything to eat or drink, Cal?' she asked politely.

'Don't worry, Lynn, I'll make myself at home—if there's anything I want, I'll get it.'

'Good.' Lynn smiled and reached to kiss him. 'Well, good night, then.'

Kirsten was pleased to note that as they all said goodnight Cal sat back down on the settee. Hopefully he was going to wait down here and allow her to use her own bedroom to change. It was the least he could do under the circumstances, she thought; after all, he was taking her room and leaving her down here on the cold, hard settee.

Her parents' bedroom was on the ground floor, but Kirsten's was up under the eaves of the house. She hurried to the wooden stairs and pushed open the door.

The room was painted white and was furnished with antiques that had been bought mostly from garage sales and lovingly restored by her father. It was really a single bedroom but her parents had put the double bed in there soon after Kirsten got married so that she and Cal would be more comfortable when they came down for weekends.

Going into that bedroom always brought back memories. It had been her room since she was eleven and her parents had moved here from Yorkshire in England. Although she had missed England at first, she had fallen immediately in love with this quaint cottage and the countryside around it and she had quickly made friends. She remembered the sleepovers when her friends had slept on the pull-out settee the giggles and the midnight feasts.

Then she remembered the laughter and the different kind of midnight feasts when she had come home for the weekend and brought Cal with her and the two of them had squashed into her single bed.

Life could change so quickly, she thought as her eyes moved over the cosy patchwork quilt. Now she couldn't even bear to sleep in the same room as him.

She picked up her case and took out her nightdress dressing gown and sponge bag. Then zipped the bag back up again and slid it beneath the bed, out of the way.

She sat down at her dressing table, emptied the content of her sponge bag and then cleansed her face. She looked tired, which was no wonder, considering the turmoil of the day and the fact she had hardly slept last night. Pulling her hair free of its pony-tail, she gave it a vigorous brush. The lifted up her nightwear and headed for the bathroom next door.

She was surprised when she walked into the bathroom to see Cal standing at the sink, shaving. He had nothing on apart from a large bath sheet wrapped around his middle

Obviously he had just come out of the shower. His honey-tanned skin gleamed with water and his hair was still damp. She tried not to allow her gaze to move over his body, but she couldn't help herself; she was only human and his physique was as perfect as ever.

She dragged her gaze away from the tautly muscled six-pack and the powerful sweep of his shoulders and tried to look him in the eye without blushing. 'I'm…I'm sorry, I didn't realise you were in here.'

'That's OK.' He grinned at her, totally unperturbed. 'I'm nearly finished.' He turned back to his reflection in the mirror, carefully running the razor under the water and then running it skilfully over the white foam. She didn't know why, but she stood there for a moment, watching him. The scene was so familiar, so normal to her…and for some bizarre reason that very familiarity was completely unsettling.

Cal looked around at her when she didn't leave, his eyes questioning.

'Sorry…sorry.' She backed out and shut the door, wondering if her face was as red as it felt. Retracing her steps to her bedroom and looking at her reflection in her dressing-table mirror, she saw with dismay that it was. She was as orange as a traffic cone.

Hell, what's the matter with me? she wondered hazily. So he has a fabulous athletic build; you've always known that. So what's the big deal?

And why was she burning up with sudden desire? She raked a hand through her hair and hated herself for even acknowledging that fact. Was it very sinful to lust over a man you didn't love? she wondered.

The bedroom door opened behind her. 'Bathroom's all yours,' Cal said, coming in.

He still had nothing on except for the towel; Kirsten averted her eyes hastily as she stood up.

The room was too small and far, far too intimate a place for the two of them. She tried to sidle past him, without watching him pulling back the covers of her patchwork quilt.

'Are you sure you're going to be OK downstairs?' he asked. 'I can always pull out the settee.'

'I'll be perfectly all right.' She reached the bedroom door and escaped outside with a sigh of relief.

''Night,' she heard him call lazily through the door.

''Night.' She went into the bathroom, closed the door and leaned back against it. A cold shower was what she needed, she thought angrily, a cold shower and medication. He was her ex-husband, he had 'Danger, I'll break your heart' written all over him in huge letters. She must be completely mad.

She wasn't quite brave enough for the cold shower. She set the temperature on medium and then sneaked back down the stairs in her nightgown, a pillow and a blanket tucked under her arm, feeling a little bit better.

Candy was lying sleeping by the dying embers of the fire. She lifted her ears and opened one eye to look at Kirsten, and she could have sworn there was a look of surprise on her canine face, a 'What on earth are you doing? You must be crazy' look. Then she closed her eye and went back to sleep.

The dog was right; she probably was crazy, Kirsten thought as she lay on the hard settee and tried to get comfortable, no mean feat on a settee only big enough for a pigmy to lie on.

She adjusted her pillow for the fifth time to try and avoid a crick in her neck and settled down again.

She thought about her dad, and prayed he would be all right. Then she thought about what he'd said to her before dinner. He'd accused her of lying to herself, of still being in love with Cal. That was utter nonsense. All right, she admitted there was still a chemistry between them, and she still found him very attractive, but that was sexual, nothing deeper. You couldn't build a life together on just good sex...although it had been very good...and she did miss i

She missed Cal as well, she acknowledged suddenly. He used to make her laugh…he used to hold her so tenderly.

She turned over again and pummelled the pillow, trying not to remember hot, steamy nights of passion upstairs in that bed where Cal was lying now…naked.

Candy started to snore.

Hell, this was torture. Kirsten sat up; she wasn't going to be able to sleep down here at all. She wondered if she would be better taking the cushions off the settee and lying on the floor? That seemed like a good idea.

She was just starting to arrange them when Candy sat up, then ambled over to her and lay down on the cushions. 'They're not for you, Candy.' Kirsten tried to push her off, but she wouldn't budge.

'Can't you sleep?' Cal's cool voice from the doorway made her jump.

'No,' she admitted, straining her eyes to see him in the dark. 'Can't you?'

'No. Your snoring was keeping me awake.'

'That wasn't me, it was Candy!'

'Are you sure?' She could hear the amusement in his tone now and realised he was teasing. 'What the heck are you doing anyway?'

'Playing musical cushions with Candy. When the music stops I'm hoping to be able to lie down.'

Cal flicked on the overhead light, making her blink. She pulled her dressing gown a little closer around her figure, feeling suddenly self-conscious. Heaven only knew what she must look like with her hair all over the place, sitting here on the floor at midnight, she thought.

Cal looked as wonderful as ever, even though his dark hair was a bit ruffled. At least he was wearing a dressing gown, she noted with relief.

'Looks like Candy has won to me,' Cal remarked with a grin as the dog raised her head to look at him, but didn't budge from the cushions.

'Yes, it does, doesn't it? Only for the fact that I know I'd sound paranoid, I'd be blaming Dad now…thinking he'd trained Candy specially to make me go upstairs with you.'

'Maybe you should just give in,' Cal suggested quietly. 'And come upstairs with me.'

Kirsten pushed at Candy's heavy body one more time, but she wouldn't budge.

'Come on, Kirsten, it's late and you're being a bit ridiculous now. You can't sleep down here.'

'Yes, you're right.' She stood up, deciding she was going to have to be adult about this. 'Are you sleeping in the bed or the pull-out settee?'

'The bed, but you can take it; I'll be a gentleman and move to the settee.'

'Better late than never,' she said drily.

'Hey! I was doing the decent thing—I came down here to get you, didn't I?'

'The decent thing would have been for you to sleep down here in the first place,' she told him tersely.

He smiled at that. 'I'm a creature of comfort, Kirsty, I have my limitations.' With that he turned around and went back upstairs.

Kirsten stood where she was for a moment, unsure if following him was the right thing to do. It seemed really odd, following him to bed…even if it was a separate bed.

Candy looked at Kirsten with her ears pricked. 'Don't look at me like that with those innocent eyes,' Kirsten told her. 'You've got a lot to answer for.'

Taking a deep breath, she switched out the light and made her way slowly back up the stairs.

Her bedroom was almost in total darkness and it took a moment for her eyes to adjust when she walked in. She could just about make out Cal in the bed-settee; he looked as if he was lying on his side, facing her bed.

Trying carefully to avoid the settee, she managed to stub

her toe on a chair and winced with pain. Then she knocked against her dressing table and a few bottles fell over.

'You sound like a baby elephant,' Cal remarked drolly from his bed. 'Why don't you just switch the light on and be done with it?'

'I'm fine,' she said stiffly. Reaching her bed, she took off her dressing gown and crawled thankfully beneath the covers. It was still warm from Cal's body and when she buried her head in towards the pillow she could smell the scent of his cologne. If she wasn't mistaken, it was the same cologne she had bought him for his birthday one year. He must like it to be still using it. She liked it herself, she thought wistfully; it was warmly sensual, a provocative reminder of its wearer.

'Do you remember the first time you brought me here for the weekend?' Cal asked her suddenly.

'Of course I do.' She rolled over onto her back and stared up into the darkness.

'We had fun, didn't we?'

She didn't answer him; instead she squeezed her eyes tightly closed and tried to prevent her mind from going down that avenue.

'Do you remember that first day we went out on the boat?'

At least he wasn't thinking about the great sex, she told herself wryly, which was where her mind had been.

'We stopped the engine and just drifted for a while on a sea that was silky smooth, not a breeze to ruffle even a few feathers, let alone a sail.' Kirsten remembered the moment vividly, the warmth of the sun, the languid sound of the water lapping against the sides of the boat. They had been so happy together then.

'And we started to dream about what we wanted from the future,' Cal remembered. 'You said you were going to concentrate on your singing career for three years then get married and have three children.'

'You said you'd like a house overlooking the ocean like this one, but with a big yacht, so you could sail around the Caribbean.' Kirsten smiled.

'That wasn't such a bad dream…you liked it so much you asked if you could sail away with me, as I recall.'

Kirsten closed her eyes as she remembered his response, whispered softly in her ear, 'I wouldn't dream of going anywhere without you…'

'Good job we couldn't see into the future and all that choppy water,' she said softly. 'I was arrogantly confident back then, thought I could control my destiny.'

'No, you weren't. You'd gone through your fair share of rejection in your career but you'd made it to the top. That takes guts.'

'Well, if there's one thing I've learnt since that conversation it's that you can't plan the future. Life has a habit of biting back.'

'Better to at least try and make plans than to drift,' Cal said softly.

She hadn't made any real plans in a long time, hadn't dared to dream… I'm drifting now, Kirsten thought. I'm alone on a sea that's wild and choppy and somewhere along the way I've dropped the compass overboard. She rolled on her side away from him. 'Goodnight, Cal.'

Sleep was elusive, yet she was so tired. Her mind raced backwards and forwards over the different conversations of the day…then lingered on that moment in the garage where she had realised how wrong she had been to underestimate what Cal had been feeling.

What was it she had said? 'Maybe you were sad for a while, but let's face it, Cal…. what happened…left you free to pursue your career.' She cringed and hated herself for those words.

'Cal, are you asleep?' She rolled over.

'No.'

'I've been thinking….'

'Always dangerous.'

'No, Cal, this is serious.' She sat up.

'What is it?' He rolled over to look across at her.

'I keep…I keep thinking about what I said to you out-side…'

He waited silently for her to continue.

'You know…when I said that Bethany dying left you free to pursue your career. I didn't mean it.' She stared over at him in the darkness.

'I know you didn't.' His voice was gentle.

'Oh, God, Cal…don't be nice to me.' She sat up in the bed. 'I don't deserve it… It was a horrible thing to say…'

He got out of bed and came to sit on the edge of hers. 'You were upset, Kirsten,' he said softly.

'That's no excuse.' Her voice wobbled precariously. 'Now when I think back about…about Bethany I'm won-dering if I didn't give proper consideration to how you were feeling…'

'Oh, for heaven's sake Kirsten—' He reached to put on the bedside light, but she caught his hand, stopping him.

'No…leave the light, let me finish. There's something I need to tell you.'

He dropped his hand back to the bed but caught hold of hers, holding it tightly.

'I never blamed you for not being with me the night Bethany died. I blamed myself.'

She was glad that it was dark and that he couldn't see her face; it made it so much easier to say those words.

'How could you blame yourself?' She heard the puzzle-ment in his voice.

'Because it was my fault.' Her voice was earnest, plead-ing with him to understand. 'Don't you see, it was all my fault? I wasn't feeling well that day and yet I told you to go, told you I was perfectly all right. If I hadn't done that…then maybe…maybe everything would have been all ight.' Tears prickled behind her eyes and started to fall.

'So you see it wasn't your fault, it was mine...' Her voice broke.

'Oh, honey, it wasn't your fault.' He reached to pull her close in against him, holding her tightly, his voice husky and gentle against her ear. 'It wasn't anyone's fault.'

'It was. If I'd gone to the hospital sooner...'

'You can't think like that.'

'There's no other way to think,' she said brokenly. 'I failed. I failed you and I failed Bethany and then I wrapped myself up in my own grief and I was selfish and I didn't even realise until today how much you were hurting and I just want to say I'm sorry—'

'Hey!' Cal cut across her firmly and held her a little bit away from him. 'Take it easy, Kirsten. You know I'm... very... very fond of this woman that you are lambasting into and I'm telling you now that she doesn't deserve to be spoken about like that.' Gently he wiped the tears away from her face. 'The Kirsten that I know doesn't have a selfish bone in her body,' he said gently. 'And she has nothing to blame herself for.'

'So why do I feel like this?'

'Because you've bottled things up too hard, too long.' He stroked her hair back from her face with a tender hand. 'And your dumb husband didn't know what to say or do to make things any better.'

She smiled shakily at that. 'Of all the adjectives in the world that I could think of to describe you, Cal, dumb wouldn't be one.'

'Don't be too nice to me now,' Cal warned, a teasing note in his voice. 'I'm not above taking advantage of the situation.'

She rested back against his chest. His dressing gown was damp from her tears and she moved, so that instead of her head lying against the material she was resting against his torso. His body felt warm and infinitely comforting. She breathed deeply, loving the scent of his skin.

It was wonderful just to be held like this…how many times over the last two years had she longed for this? she wondered hazily.

She slipped her hand beneath the material and stroked over his ribs, then higher towards his shoulders, feeling the powerful network of muscles that tensed beneath her touch.

'Kirsten.' She heard the note of warning in his husky tone, but hazily decided to ignore it.

'Kirsten…?'

'Maybe I don't mind you taking advantage of this situation, Cal…' she murmured. 'Just for old times' sake…just for tonight.'

She raised her head and met his lips. She tasted the softness of them tentatively. He didn't return her kiss immediately and she groaned with a kind of pent-up longing that came from the very depths of her soul as she pressed closer to him, her hands stroking the dressing gown back.

'Make love to me, Cal,' she whispered brokenly. 'I need to feel warmth…I need you.'

She kissed him again, and this time he kissed her back with a fierce need. The sensation made the pit of her stomach dip with sensual desire so heavy that her body seemed to scream for him.

She leaned back against the pillows and felt his hands stroking against the satin material of her nightdress, pulling it upwards and then over her head with an impatience that ignited a wild thrill of excitement inside her.

She was no longer thinking coherently; she was just dealing in desire, allowing her mind to switch off from everything except the touch and the taste and the scent of him. For so long she had felt nothing, any needs buried so deep she had almost denied their reality in the first place. But now she felt as if she was coming alive again as warmth and feeling sizzled through her body like the first rays of sun after a long, cold winter.

His hands stroked over her body and caressed silkily over

her breasts, until she felt them tighten and harden beneath his fingers.

He groaned and bent his head to them and a dart of red-hot fire struck through her as his mouth moved to cover them, licking and tasting her so that she moaned with a desire that was so extreme it was agonisingly blissful.

His dressing gown had been discarded and he was lying over her, his naked body touching every part of her. She felt the power of his body, felt as if she wanted to melt into him, become him, as she writhed in his arms, her hands stroking down over his back, loving the feel of his skin and the sheer majesty of his body.

They were lying sideways across the bed now. She was aware of her head hanging over the side and he slid his hands under her waist and pulled her firmly down so that she was directly under him again.

She shuddered as he moved inside her, closing her eyes on a wave of emotion so intense it threatened to drown her.

Cal was a masterful lover. He had always known how to turn her on, exactly how to make her gasp with exhilaration and tremble with need. She had almost forgotten the wild excitement of being in his arms.

As he moved against her he kissed her, his movements slow and teasing. His hands cupped her breasts, his fingers tantalising her.

'That feels so good.' She murmured the words against him, reaching for his mouth, running her fingers through his hair, loving the texture and the feel of him, the drugging hardness of his body and the tantalising sensuality of his kiss.

Then suddenly his movements stilled and he pulled back from her, and the shock and the disappointment were almost as great as the pleasure of a few moments ago.

'Cal...?'

'Tell me again that you want me,' he commanded huskily.

She sat up slightly so that her breasts were pressed against the rough hair of his chest. 'I want you so much it hurts.'

She didn't want him to stop, her body was crying out for satisfaction, and it was an ache so deep that it overruled all other sensible thoughts.

He kissed her again, a sensual, intoxicating kiss that turned her to liquid inside. She reached out and put his hands back on her breasts, willing him to continue, to stroke her, to caress her, to make her feel whole again.

Then he was inside her again and his movements became fervid, forceful, taking her with a dominance that sent waves of pleasure lapping through her body.

CHAPTER EIGHT

SUNLIGHT filtered through the blinds on Kirsten's bedroom window and played softly over the room. She heard the birds singing outside and the faint sound of music coming from somewhere and for a while she lay there without opening her eyes.

Kirsten couldn't remember the last time she had felt this good…this happy. Her whole body was tingling with a feeling of well-being. She stretched sleepily and moved so that she could cuddle in against Cal, her hand reaching out for him. But she was reaching into an empty space. She opened her eyes and looked across at the other side of the bed. Cal was gone.

She sat up and looked around the room, but she was on her own. The clock on the bedside table said nine-thirty. Kirsten hadn't slept this late in ages, but it was no wonder after the blissful exertions of the night. Cal had brought her to the heights of ecstasy more than once before they had fallen asleep locked in each other's arms.

Just thinking about it now made her heart flip with sensual desire.

She forced her mind away from their lovemaking for a moment and thought about the conversation they'd had about Bethany. She was glad they had talked about that. She felt renewed…at peace with herself about what had happened for the first time in two years.

Now all she had to do was make some sense of her turbulent feelings for Cal.

Her thoughts in that department were so muddled that she couldn't begin to start untangling them. Just remem-

122

bering his body against hers sent shivers of wonder racing through her.

It had been an incredible night, so much tenderness and passion…yet not one word of love, she reminded herself, and frowned. What did she expect? Of course there had been no words of love… Cal didn't love her and she…well, she was long over that particular emotion.

Suddenly she remembered Cal telling her last night that he was very *fond* of her. She didn't know why that should upset her now. It hadn't seemed to matter at the time, because she had been so distraught and distracted and he had been so gentle and wonderful…

Oh, God…had she thrown herself at him? she wondered suddenly.

She remembered him pulling back from her for just one moment as he paused to think about what they were doing. When she analysed it now, she knew that was what he had been doing, Cal always thought everything through. In the heat of any moment he was always controlled…it was one of the things that she had always liked about him. Where she acted impulsively, he was level-headed.

He'd certainly been thinking clearly when they made love. He'd even checked with her that it was what she wanted before going the whole way…she had almost begged him to continue.

And they hadn't used any contraception.

Idiot! Total, foolish idiot! she berated herself fiercely, hardly able to believe her own stupidity.

Kirsten flung the bedclothes back, so angry with herself that she couldn't bear even to think about it a moment longer.

She went through to the bathroom to shower. Even standing under the heavy flow of water, she couldn't wash away the panic of her thoughts. Had Cal assumed that she was on the Pill when she had asked him to continue…?

The thought of facing Cal settled like a heavy weight

around her. She felt embarrassed and foolish and she didn't know what she was going to say to him. But the sooner she faced him the better, she told herself, stepping out of the warm water and reaching for a towel.

A little while later, dressed in a pair of faded denim jeans and a pink T-shirt and wearing a lot more make-up than usual to cover the pallor of her skin, Kirsten made her way downstairs.

The music she had been able to hear in her bedroom was her mother's radio, which was blaring out to an empty kitchen.

'Mum…?' Kirsten put her head around the door to the lounge. There was no one in there either. The room was neat and tidy, the cushions placed back where they should be on the settee.

Kirsten retraced her steps to the kitchen and then noticed the note propped up against the kettle.

Taken your father into town for his check-up. Cal is outside doing a few jobs for us—will you bring him a cup of coffee? See you later.
Love, Mum.

She put the note down and glanced out of the kitchen window. Sure enough, Cal was down by the jetty. He was chopping wood, working without pausing, throwing the neatly cut blocks into a pile beside Candy, who was sitting watching him.

Kirsten flicked on the kettle and got two mugs out of the cupboard. What could she say to him about last night? She rehearsed a few lines in her mind; all of them sounded wrong.

Deciding to wing it and see what he said first, she poured the coffee and brought his outside.

All the rain and mist of yesterday had melted away into a glorious spring day; a warm breeze ruffled the silky blue of the ocean and rustled through the trees.

Cal was sitting on an upturned log with his back to her, looking out over the ocean. She thought at first he was just having a rest, but as she came closer she realised he was talking to someone on his mobile phone.

'How does it feel to be back in sunny California?' he asked, and then laughed at whatever the reply had been. 'Well, I'm glad you're back.'

Who was he talking to? Kirsten wondered, stopping just a few feet away from him. She should have alerted him to her presence because he obviously hadn't heard her, but something…probably nosiness, made her hesitate.

'When are you arriving in San Francisco? Really? Well, I can't wait. You've got my address there, haven't you?' Again he gave that low, husky, sensual laugh that turned Kirsten's insides to jelly. He had to be talking to a woman.

'Is Brian coming with you?' he asked, and suddenly Kirsten knew all too clearly whom Cal was speaking to.

'Well, that's a bit of good news. OK, Maeve, I'll look forward to it.'

If it was good news then obviously Brian wasn't coming, Kirsten thought derisively, and then hated herself for giving a damn.

She took a step backwards, and Candy looked up and bounded over to say hello, making Cal glance around.

He smiled at her gently and stood up. 'Listen, I'm going to have to go,' he said to Maeve. 'Yeah…sure, we'll do that.'

Cal snapped the mobile closed and walked over to Kirsten. He looked extremely sexy this morning, she noted. Yet he was only dressed casually in denim jeans and a blue shirt, the sleeves rolled back in an attempt to keep him cool.

'Good morning,' he drawled lazily. 'Or should I say, good afternoon?'

'It's not that late.' She tried to keep her composure, but when she met his blue eyes all she could think about was last night.

'I'm sorry I interrupted your phone conversation.'

'That's OK, it was just a friend,' he said easily.

'No one I'd know, then?' she asked casually.

Cal just smiled. 'More to the point, how are you this morning?'

He wasn't about to tell her who it was. Maybe because he suspected she knew the truth...that Maeve was much more than just a friend.

It's none of your business any more, Kirsten reminded herself angrily.

She was really glad she had left her hair loose, and that the breeze caught hold of it at that moment, ruffling it slightly over her face. She had never felt more discomfited, more like hiding herself away.

'I'm OK. I brought you a coffee.' She held the drink out to him like some kind of barricade that she wanted to keep between them.

'Thanks.'

As he reached to take it from her their fingers touched and she felt her heart slamming against her chest, confirming the lie that she was OK...she was far from that.

She needed to say something about last night to cover her embarrassment, but what?

'It's a lovely morning, isn't it?' she heard herself say lightly.

He smiled.

'Have I said something amusing?' she asked, distracted by the glint of humour in his eyes.

'No...just sometimes you sound very English...they always talk about the weather, don't they, to cover all gaps in the conversation?'

She smiled. He was right, she was stalling; she'd rather talk about anything right now than the minefield of las night. She took a deep breath, and, unable to bear the tension inside her a moment longer, blurted out, 'Listen, about last night…'

It was only after she had spoken that she realised that he had said the exact same thing at the same time.

Their eyes met and he grinned ruefully. 'Sorry…you go first.'

Why hadn't she kept her big mouth closed and let him do the talking? she asked herself wretchedly.

'Well…' She averted her eyes from his gaze. 'I just wanted to say that last night…last night was…I was upset…and you were very comforting…' Hell, did that sound as pathetic as she thought it did?

She risked a glance up at him and he met her gaze with a raised eyebrow. 'Comforting?' he repeated sardonically.

'Yes…'

He sipped his coffee and looked so coolly collected that she felt even more on edge. She longed for him to say something, be a gentleman and help her out of this. 'Anyway…' she continued when he said nothing. 'It was good that we were able to talk—'

'Yes, it was.' He interrupted her at last, his voice low and husky. 'And what happened between us was extremely pleasurable; it brought back a lot of happy memories of the way we used to be together.'

'Yes, well, one thing we always had in abundance was passion,' she said uneasily.

He frowned. 'You say that with a hint of contempt in your voice, but surely passion is the one great ingredient of any relationship—'

'Not…not on its own,' she cut across him fiercely.

She waited for him to deny that…but he didn't. Maybe she should respect him for that, she told herself; at least he wasn't trying to pretend that last night had anything to do with love…he wasn't that big a hypocrite.

Desperately she tried to maintain her pride and at the

same time remain sensible. 'Look, I meant what I said last night...about being sorry...you know, for what I said about your feelings and Bethany...' She struggled to gather her thoughts and looked up at him, her eyes filled with earnest entreaty. 'And...and I'm glad we talked about it. We needed some closure on all that pain.'

'Yes, we did.'

She nodded. 'I think it helped...I'm hoping we can put all that...stuff behind us now?'

He looked around and she realised he was going to put the cup down somewhere. She didn't want him to do that...if he reached to give her a hug or touched her in any way she didn't know how she would handle it.

Hastily she took a step backwards from him. 'I think we should just look at last night as a final period of mourning. We were both a bit emotional...it was that, Cal, that...fired what happened. But we've made our peace and now we need to get on with the future. You've got...' She nodded to the mobile phone in his shirt pocket, unable even to say a name. 'You've got women queuing up for you, I'm sure. And I have to think about...what I want.'

'And what do you want?' Cal asked her very quietly.

'Well...' She really struggled now. The truth was, right at this moment she hadn't got a clue what she wanted. All she needed was to escape with some pride intact, but how could she do that and at the same time tell him there was nothing serious in her life? 'Jason and I are going to meet up next week and—'

'Jason?' Cal frowned. 'Look, Kirsten...I think Jason's a mistake.'

'Really?' Kirsten stared at him. How dared he say that to her? What right had he to preach about mistakes when he was in love with a married woman?

'Well, I don't know where you're coming from on that Jason's single, and he cares a lot about me.' She shrugged

'But frankly, Cal, it's none of your damn business,' she said bluntly.

'Look, I'm only saying this because I care about you.'

'Well, don't.'

'Don't what? Care what happens to you? Or say something?'

'Both.' Her voice trembled precariously. She didn't want a man who just 'cared' about her. Who was 'fond' of her.

'I have to say something, Kirsten. OK, maybe last night was…down to us getting emotional…we got carried away. Maybe I should have stopped. But I didn't.'

She didn't say anything to that. The truth was, she could have stopped him, should have stopped him. But instead she had thrown herself at him.

'What happens if you're pregnant?' he asked suddenly.

She stared at him, the question making her heart hammer against her chest fiercely.

He threw his coffee away onto the grass and put the cup down. 'Look, Kirsten.' There was an expression of determination suddenly in Cal's eyes, and he took a step forward. 'If you are pregnant—'

She moved back so hastily from him she nearly fell over on the uneven grass. 'I'm not!'

He reached out and caught hold of her arm, steadying her. The grip of his hand seemed to burn through her skin. 'You don't know that for sure. We got carried away, Kirsten, and we need to face up to that now.'

'Yes, we got carried away.' She repeated his words numbly. 'It's a mistake I'll think about if…and when I have to. Until then I suggest we just treat it as if it never happened.'

She turned away from him, tears stinging her eyes.

Cal was going to follow her back into the house, and then changed his mind. Instead he turned and picked up the axe again.

He'd made a damn mess of that, he thought angrily. All

the theories he'd had about getting Kirsten to open up to him and talk about the past had just backfired in his face.

She had said they should look on last night as closure.

Closure on the pain of the past was definitely what he wanted, but he had hoped it would herald the start of a new beginning, not signal the end. He struck through the pieces of wood with more venom than was strictly necessary.

Maybe he'd rushed things too much. He'd always been too damn impatient for his own good. Maybe talking about the past had made Kirsten think about the future and she had decided she was in love with Jason?

'Jason and I are meeting next week.' Her words drummed through him. Jason wasn't right for her and he'd prove it to her if it was the last thing he did, he thought, smashing through another piece of wood.

When Kirsten went back into the house she was so upset she didn't know what to do with herself. She snapped off the cheerful, inane music coming from the radio and paced around the kitchen for a moment before going out into the hallway and picking up the telephone. She'd ring Chloe, she thought. What she needed right now was a good dose of her friend's cheerful common sense.

But Chloe wasn't in and all she got was her own voice on the answering machine. She hung up and on impulse started to phone Jason. Halfway through dialling, she hung up. She didn't want to speak to Jason; what she wanted to do was go outside and throw herself into Cal's arms.

But that wasn't an option, she told herself fiercely. Cal didn't love her. And if she threw herself at him again…let's face it, the way she had last night…she would be going back full circle, making the same mistake she'd made three years ago.

She remembered reading somewhere that life was a test. That you were sent through it to learn your lesson and unti l you did you were forced to go back, making the same mistakes again and again.

Well, she'd learnt her lesson, she told herself shakily, and she had learnt it the hard way…she couldn't go back and open herself up to that heartache again. She wouldn't be pregnant, she told herself sternly. And if she was then she'd face that challenge on her own, not in a loveless relationship.

The sound of her parents' car drawing up outside was a welcome relief. She'd think about everything later, she told herself fiercely.

Kirsten's parents persuaded them to stay and have some lunch before setting off for San Francisco. They were in an ebullient mood as they returned from town. The results of her father's latest tests showed that he was making a good recovery, and the relief that they all felt was palpable in the atmosphere, successfully masking the tension that lay between Kirsten and Cal.

'They think it's the medication and the fact that I've been doing what I'm told,' Robert said jovially. 'But really it's the love of a good woman that's fixing me up.'

'Please, Bob, you're making me feel quite embarrassed,' Lynn said. 'If you come out with any more slushy lines like that I'm going to really start worrying about you.'

Despite the no-nonsense tone, Kirsten saw the look of happiness in her mother's eyes as she got up from the dining-room table.

Her parents were like different people today, she thought. It was amazing how a piece of good news could make you look better; her father actually appeared stronger already.

She glanced across the table at Cal. Since she had left him outside he had been busy all morning. Considering the fact that they didn't get much in the way of cold weather, there were enough logs in the shed now to see her parents through two years, and he had fixed the bolt on the back door as well. She watched as he laughed at one of her father's jokes and something inside her twisted and curved out of all recognition.

Cal glanced up and caught her eye. I'm still in love with him, she thought suddenly.

The reality struck her bodily like some kind of an electric shock from absolutely nowhere. Her first instinct was denial. She didn't love him…she was over him. What the hell was the matter with her?

He smiled at her gently and it was as if someone had closed a gate on her, trapping her with no other way to go. She did love him! She'd always loved him! Her heart froze and then raced as cold and hot waves of fear and panic struck into her.

Was it only a few hours ago that she had been reassuring herself that she had learnt her lesson about Cal? And yet here she was, admitting she loved him! Loving Cal had led to such heartache; she couldn't go through that again…she just couldn't.

'Well, I suppose we should be on our way,' he said suddenly.

She nodded. She definitely wanted to get away, but not with Cal; she wanted to run away from him in the opposite direction as far as she could get.

As Kirsten said goodbye to her mother she noticed her dad taking Cal to one side.

She strained her ears to hear what it was they said but to no avail.

'Take care,' Lynn said reaching to give her a hug. 'And give Cal another chance,' she whispered against her ear before she released her.

She didn't have any time to answer that because Cal had come over. 'Thanks for everything, Lynn,' he said, reaching to give her a hug.

How easy they are around each other, Kirsten thought, watching. How warm and natural.

How could she give Cal another chance when, by the sounds of that phone call she had overheard this morning, things were just the same between him and Maeve?

Maybe it suited Cal to compartmentalise his life. Have a mistress on one hand for excitement and love…and a partner on the other to fill in the gaps and provide a family…but it certainly didn't suit her.

The very idea was abhorrent to her. She couldn't survive in a triangle relationship like that. It was all or nothing for her.

Her father came over and hugged her tightly. ''Bye, sweetheart; you take care of each other, you hear?'

'Do you want me to drive, Kirsten?' Cal asked as they made their way outside towards the car.

She was going to say no and then with a shrug she handed the keys over. She'd done enough driving yesterday and she felt she needed to just switch off now.

The last glimpse they had of her parents was as they stood arm in arm waving them goodbye from the porch.

'At least it was good news for your dad this morning,' Cal remarked as he turned the car onto the open road. 'I told you he was made of strong stuff.'

'Yes, it's a relief.' She watched Cal's hands on the steering wheel, strong and capable, and remembered them on her body, remembered taking them and putting them over her breasts, inviting his caresses, begging him to continue making love to her.

She closed her eyes on a red-hot wave of desire.

'Are you tired?' Cal looked around at her.

'A bit…' she lied.

'Listen, Kirsten, about this morning—'

'Let's just leave that well alone, Cal,' she said immediately. 'I think we both said too much.'

He inclined his head. 'You're probably right.'

'We should go through those notes that Theo gave us.' She forced herself to sound businesslike.

'I think we'll forget about them,' Cal said drily. 'At least until tomorrow.'

Kirsten looked across at him with a raised eyebrow. 'Excuse me, but did I just hear the great perfectionist himself sound half-hearted about his homework?' she tried to joke. 'That's not like you?'

'Isn't it?' Cal's voice was coolly indifferent. 'Perhaps you don't know me as well as you think you do.'

Kirsten frowned and looked away from him out at the passing scenery. She knew him well enough, she told herself firmly. She knew he was in love with a woman who would only bring him heartache. Maeve didn't really love him; if she did she could never stay married to Brian, no matter how it helped her career.

They drove the rest of the way in silence.

Kirsten must have fallen asleep because she was startled when Cal reached out and touched her arm.

'Kirsten, we're here. We're in San Francisco.'

She looked up to see that he was pulling the car to a halt outside a row of terrace houses.

'Is this where I'm to stay?' She looked over towards the terrace of waterfront houses.

'Yep, that's it.' He pointed to the middle house. It was painted white with grey shutters on the windows and looked like an old-fashioned doll's house.

'I'll get your luggage.' Cal got out and went around the back of the car. 'You go and let yourself in.'

Kirsten picked up her handbag and found the front-door key and then, lifting Theo's notes, she climbed out of the car.

Daylight was starting to fade now and the lights on the bay twinkled in a rosy pink glow of sunset. She could hear the clanging musical noise of the cable cars coming from the end of the road as she opened the gate in the white picket fence and walked up the path to the front door.

She smiled as she noticed the mat saying 'Home Swee

Home'. Quickly she pushed her key in the lock and walked in. It took a moment to find the light switch and then the darkness was replaced by warm subdued lighting that reflected on polished wooden floors and beautiful antique furniture.

'Is it OK?' Cal followed her into the lounge a moment later.

'It's more than OK,' she told him, stroking a loving hand over a writing bureau as she moved to look through a doorway into a very stylish white kitchen. 'I might never want to leave this place.'

Cal smiled. 'Shall I take your suitcase upstairs for you?'

'Thanks.' She followed him back out to the hall and up the narrow stairs.

There were two bedrooms, each very cosily and simply decorated in a modern style. 'I expected the studio to put me in a serviceable apartment. This place is lovely,' Kirsten said in astonishment.

'Well, they like to look after their leading ladies,' Cal said with a grin as he put her suitcase in the master bedroom at the front of the house.

Kirsten moved past him to look out of the window. 'I've even got a view of the bay!'

'Well, after commandeering your bedroom first last night, I though the least I could do was give you the best room tonight.'

'What do you mean?' Kirsten whirled around to look at him. 'Where exactly are you staying…?'

'Why, the smaller room across the corridor, of course.'

'You are joking?'

'No.' He shrugged. 'You don't think the studio would splash out and put you in here all on your own, do you?'

'Do you know, for one wild moment I thought they had,' she said sardonically. 'Silly me! Why would they do something as decent as that when they can make us double up and get such wonderful PR mileage out of it?'

'Why, indeed?' For a second Cal grinned at her.

'Well, it's just an impossible situation. You realise that, don't you?'

'No.' Cal shrugged. 'Why is it an impossible situation? We'll be out working most of the day anyway.'

'That's not the point, Cal.'

'Isn't it?' His mobile phone rang and he turned away, answering it as he went downstairs. 'Oh, hi; yes, I'm in town now…'

Who was that? she wondered, sinking down onto the bed beside her. Another woman waiting for him in the wings?

She buried her head in her hands as she tried to think clearly. It was only the fact that she was tired, short of money and in a town she didn't know that well that stopped her from picking up her bag and walking out of here to a hotel.

'Kirsten, do you want a sandwich or something? The fridge is well stocked,' Cal called up the stairs to her.

'No, I don't, thank you,' she yelled back.

'OK…well, do you want first shower or shall I? There's only one bathroom, remember?'

If someone up in heaven was playing a joke on her, then she didn't think this was very funny, she thought as she got up from the bed. 'Yes, I'll have the first shower,' she replied, before slamming her bedroom door closed.

Tomorrow she was getting in contact with the studio with the producer, with the highest authority she could find and asking them to move her out of here, she told herself firmly.

CHAPTER NINE

KIRSTEN pulled the curtains back from her bedroom window just as dawn broke.

She stood for a long time and watched as the sky changed from misty darkness to a flamingo-pink and then eggshell-blue, each of the colours seeping across the sea like a batik work of art. Her eyes moved from the distant red of the Golden Gate Bridge to the fishing boats that bobbed serenely out at anchor from the wharf.

This place would be paradise if it weren't for the fact that she had to share it, she thought, turning away from the view. Despite all her best efforts to get the studio to relocate her, she had been in the house with Cal for nearly two weeks.

She couldn't honestly say that it had been too perturbing an experience; they had been working such long hours that there had been no time to get in each other's way, or think too deeply about anything else. But it was an awkward situation, especially as Kirsten felt her blood pressure racing every time they touched, every time they so much as looked at each other. It was bad enough having to work with him all day, but that she should have to return to the same house at night with him as well was as much as flesh and blood could stand.

Today was the start of their first weekend off and Kirsten was planning on spending it finding somewhere else to stay. If the studio wouldn't move her then there was nothing else for it; she would have to dip into her meagre savings and move herself.

She put her dressing gown on over her pyjamas and cautiously opened her bedroom door.

Cal's bedroom door was wide open and she had a clear view of his bed. It was perfectly made, as if it had never been slept in. Of course, if there was any decency about the man he wouldn't have slept in it, he'd have gone and got a hotel immediately after they'd found themselves stuck here together, she thought.

She hesitated as the idea struck her that maybe he hadn't come home last night. They had been taking separate vehicles to the studio each morning. Kirsten had insisted that she wanted to be able to arrive and leave under her own steam. Usually Cal was home before her, but not last night.

She'd gone straight to bed and hadn't thought about it, but now that she did she realised that she had fallen asleep before she heard him come in.

Curiously she went across the landing and peeped around the doorframe into his room.

'Looking for something?' Cal's voice, coming from the bathroom behind her, startled her.

'I thought maybe you'd moved out,' she murmured, trying not to notice the fact that he was just freshly out of the shower and that all he was wearing was a towel around his middle.

'No, as you can see, I'm still here.' He smiled. 'It's nice to have some time off, isn't it? What are you planning on doing today?'

'I'm flat-hunting,' she told him.

'Isn't that a waste of time when you've got perfectly reasonable accommodation here?'

'But it's not reasonable, is it, Cal, to expect an ex-husband and -wife to share a house?'

'So we were married once? So what?' Cal shrugged 'We're civilised about it; we're friends.'

She hesitated. It was hard to think that she could ever just be a friend with Cal. Her emotions were too deeply involved. Her eyes flicked down over his body, allowing herself just one second to assimilate how virile, how over-whelmingly attractive he was.

'I just don't feel comfortable with the situation, Cal. So I'm moving out.'

'Well, if that's how you feel...' Cal shrugged. 'Tell you what, as I'm at a loose end this morning, I'll come and help you find a flat.'

Kirsten frowned. 'If you told me that *you* were going to look for a flat then maybe you'd be making some kind of acceptable proposition.'

'We're only here for another few months...I don't see the point. Besides, I like it here. It's real handy for work.'

In other words, she was the unreasonable one, it was her problem and she'd have to deal with it, she thought angrily. 'Are you finished with the bathroom? Because I want to have a shower. I've got a lot to do today.'

'Sure.' He stepped to one side to let her pass. 'Would you like some breakfast? I'm going to go down to that French bakery at the end of the street and get some fresh bread and croissants—'

'No, thanks, Cal.'

As she moved past him her eyes drifted again to his chest, to the tight muscles of his stomach, and it took all her will power not to reach out and touch him. Closing the door hurriedly behind her, she leaned back against it. The sooner she was out of here the better, she told herself for the millionth time.

Kirsten dressed in a pair of dark jeans with a sparkle of embroidery along the sides, pulled on a fitted turquoise top, and left her hair loose around her shoulders.

Cal was just back from the shop when she went down-stairs.

'Sure you don't want something to eat?' he asked as he put his purchases down on the counter top.

She shook her head. 'No, I'm just going to have fruit juice and coffee, thanks.'

'Are you feeling OK?'

The casually asked question made her nervous. Was he wondering if she was pregnant? 'I'm fine,' she said airily. 'I've never been one for breakfast, remember?'

'Yes…I remember.' He smiled at her. It was a smile that played havoc with all her strength and her resolve to distance herself from him as soon as possible.

'Is this fresh coffee in the pot?' She turned away from him to get herself a cup.

'Yes. Will you pour me a cup as well?'

Silently she did as he asked. This was a dangerous situation, she told herself sharply. It was too cosy, too reminiscent of past times before all the pain and realisations of mistakes. And that was why she had to leave, because this was an illusion.

'Did you go somewhere nice last night?' she asked, bringing the drinks over to the table.

'I just had a few drinks in town.'

Did that mean Maeve had arrived in San Francisco? If Brian wasn't with her it would explain Cal's absence last night.

That was the reality of this situation, she reminded herself as she sat down.

'I bought a local paper while I was out and had a glance through the accommodation section,' Cal said as he carried a plate of buttered croissants to the table and sat down opposite her.

'On your own behalf or mine?'

He flashed her that blue-eyed 'What do you think?' look and she shrugged. 'Can't blame a girl for hoping.'

He lifted the paper from the seat beside him and she noticed it was folded over at the columns of houses to rent. 'There's one here that sounds good.' He read it out.

It sounded wonderful, but when he read the price she nearly fell over in shock.

'What do you think?' He glanced over at her.

'Too expensive, Cal,' she murmured.

'But the area is good.'

She shook her head and he read on.

She really couldn't afford any of those, she thought as she listened. The studio had as yet only paid her a small retainer and most of it had gone to pay her overdraft at the bank.

'I need something much smaller,' she said, cutting across him in mid-flow. 'A small apartment is about all I can afford at the moment.'

'What do you mean?' Cal asked casually as he got up from the table to take his plate over for another croissant.

'Just what I said.'

'Come on, Kirsten, you must be able to afford something better. You haven't been out of work for long, have you? And you had a successful run on Broadway. Plus that TV show.'

Kirsten looked over at him. He was standing with his back to her, pouring himself another cup of coffee. She didn't know whether to admit the truth and tell him her agent had ripped her off and she had only just finished getting out of the legal mire of debt. Or just ignore the question.

If she told him the truth he'd probably say, I told you so, and he'd be right. She hated that.

'Would you like another coffee?' Cal asked turning and holding up the pot to her.

She nodded and he brought it over to the table with him.

'So what's the problem, Kirsten?' he asked gently as he retook his seat and reached to pour her drink.

'The problem is that the studio won't move me,' she prevaricated. 'I've tried to go through all the regular channels and people keep shifting me over, telling me to speak to someone else in another department, and when I try that the person is either unavailable or unable to help and transfers me through to another department.'

'I see.' Cal sipped his coffee and leaned back in his chair.

'I've even attempted to speak to whoever is at the top of the production company, but everything just meets with a blank wall and I'm pushed sideways again.'

'I see.'

Kirsten leaned forward suddenly. 'Have you ever heard of Sugar Productions?

'Of course I've heard of them; they're making our film.'

'Yes, but they're a new company, aren't they?'

'So I believe.'

'Do you know who's in charge? Because nobody seems to know for sure…all I need is the name of the guy who is pulling the strings.'

'I know quite a lot of people up there,' Cal told her steadily.

'Maybe you could have a word, then?' She looked over at him hopefully. 'Maybe someone in the know up there could move me?'

'Maybe,' Cal said easily.

She stared at him and then smiled. She should have asked him two weeks ago. It was obvious he would know people at the top; Cal knew everyone. 'It would be great if you could.'

Cal looked away from her towards the paper. 'In the meantime, are you going to tell me why you can't afford decent accommodation?'

'Well, I'm still paying my share of the rent in LA, of course…' She hesitated and then let her breath out in a sigh. 'I might as well tell you, Cal…that agent that you were asking me about ages ago, Chandler…well, he ripped me off and left me with a lot of debt.' She looked across at him, waiting for him to say the words 'I told you so'.

He didn't say anything for a moment. 'When you say he ripped you off, how much are we talking?' he asked cautiously. ' A little or a lot?'

'I think the word I'd use is, completely.' She took a deep

breath and looked across at him. 'I know what you're going to say, and before you do I'll say it for you; yes, it's my own fault, and, yes, I was a damn fool.'

'I wasn't going to say that,' Cal said quietly.

'Well, you'd be right to say it.' She pushed her chair back from the table and raked her hands through her hair. 'I just wasn't thinking straight at the time; our divorce was going through and I was...' She glanced over at him. 'I was in a mess and I signed contracts I should never have signed.'

She watched his eyes darken. 'You should have told me.'

'And what would you have done?' She shrugged. 'Apart from anything else, by the time I'd found out about Chandler it was too late, the money was gone. And you were about to become my ex-husband. I could hardly expect you to bail me out. You'd already agreed a generous settlement—which, incidentally, went to Chandler as well.'

'You still should have told me. I'd have helped you, Kirsten.'

'I know, but maybe that's why I didn't tell you.' She stood up from the table and turned away from him to stand at the kitchen sink, pretending to get herself a glass of water. 'We were separated and I had to stand on my own two feet. If you want the truth, that was why I didn't take your calls just before our divorce went through; I didn't want you to know I'd made such a mess—'

'I thought it was because you were with Jason Giles. You did a lot of running around with him after I left.'

She turned to look at him then. 'And you were living like a monk in London, I suppose?' she muttered sarcastically, remembering that awful time.

He shook his head and got up from the table. 'No. I won't lie to you, Kirsten. There were other women.'

'I know. I read all about them in the papers. They even managed to link you with Maeve.'

He came across towards her. 'I thought you didn't read that kind of stuff.'

Kirsten shrugged helplessly.

'I'm sorry if I hurt you, Kirsten.'

She shrugged again and hoped he wasn't going to come any closer to her, because a kind of weakness had started to invade her body. A need to be held by him became so urgently demanding that it set all alarms bells ringing. 'Well, I guess we both did our fair share of inflicting hurt.' She tried to sound offhand. As if she was past any recriminations. But it was a lie; the memory of him and Maeve locked in each other's arms still haunted her, still inflicted as much pain as it had ever done.

'Listen, I can't stand here talking all day.' She moved away from him and started to clear away the dishes from the table. 'I've got things to do. And...and Jason's flying in today.'

'Is he?' Cal leaned back against the sink, watching her.

'Yes, he's taking me for dinner.'

'Very nice.'

'Yes.' She smiled at him over-brightly.

'So if you are doing dinner with Jason, how about lunch with me?' he asked suddenly.

She hesitated and then shook her head. 'That would be no good for my figure at all, Cal.'

'There's nothing wrong with your figure,' Cal drawled huskily.

There was something very sexy about the way he said that, something that made her turn warm inside. But then she thought everything about Cal was sexy...he just oozed that particular quality. That was why she had to keep her distance.

'Thanks, Cal, but I've got too much on.'

'Apartment-hunting?'

'Yes.' She was going to put her cup in the sink and then

finding that he was blocking the way, she diverted to the other side of the counter.

'Well... Tell you what,' he drawled lazily, 'I'll have a word with the powers that be about a new place if you have lunch with me.'

She glanced over at him sharply. 'Have the studio suggested we have lunch together? Because this is getting out of hand, Cal; all this PR business is—'

'The studio haven't suggested it,' Cal cut across her swiftly. 'No catches, no hidden agenda, it's just lunch.' He spread his hands in appeal. 'Humour me.'

When he looked at her like that she would have done anything for him. And the thought of going out for lunch with him was a pleasant one... 'And you'll have a word with the studio?' she asked cautiously.

He nodded.

'OK, lunch sounds like a good idea.' She paused and then grinned. 'Of course, a better idea would be for you to look at one of those houses that you were reading about in the paper. I'll help you if you want?'

'Don't push your luck, Kirsten,' Cal muttered drolly.

She turned away with a smile. 'Lunch it is, then.'

It was a glorious day, warm and sunny with not a hint of a cloud in the sky. Cal put the top down on his Mercedes and they drove down to the wharf and then strolled along by the sea.

There was a companionable silence between them for a while. As if they were both content just to relax after the pressures of the last few weeks.

'How's your dad?' Cal asked as they stopped to watch some fishermen repairing their nets.

'He's fine. I rang when I got home last night. He and Mum were on great form. They're planning a cruise.'

'They'll enjoy that.' Cal smiled. 'I've got those football

tickets, by the way…so tell your dad next time you're talking to him.'

'That's very kind of you, Cal.' She paused.

'I can sense the word ''but'' coming into this conversation.' Cal grinned and turned to look at her. 'Don't worry,
I'm not being kind. I want to go to that football game
anyway. I've already settled it with Theo.'

'Have you? You don't seem to have the same problem
I have when it comes to sorting things out with the studio,'
she reflected.

'Let's not talk about work,' Cal said, his eyes flicking
over her thoughtfully. 'I've had enough of the studio and
filming for a while.'

'So have I,' she agreed.

'Good. So where do you fancy eating? I don't mind telling you that my stomach is complaining of a lack of food.'

'After all those croissants?' she teased.

'I'm a big guy.' Cal grinned at her. 'Got to keep my
strength up. So, where do you fancy going?'

'I don't mind. I don't know San Francisco all that well,
so you choose.'

'Well. Obviously it's a good place for seafood. And I
know a restaurant that does the best clam chowder you've
ever tasted. How does that sound?'

'It sounds great.' She smiled.

The restaurant Cal brought her to had fabulous views out
over the bay. Because it wasn't very busy they were seated
at one of the best tables in the window and the waiter
handed them some menus and retreated.

There was silence between them as Kirsten studied the
menu. When she put it down she was a bit disconcerted to
find Cal leaning back in his chair, watching her.

'Sorry, are you ready to order?' She hurriedly picked up
the menu again. 'There's such a large selection I'm spoilt
for choice.'

'Take your time. We're not in any hurry.' Cal summoned

the waiter and ordered some wine. 'Chardonnay all right?' He checked with Kirsten.

'Yes.' She smiled. 'But just one glass, otherwise I won't be able to drink tonight.'

'You could always ring Jason, tell him you'll see him tomorrow,' Cal suggested lightly.

Kirsten shook her head. 'No, I've told him tonight is fine. Besides, he's going back to LA tomorrow morning.'

'I see…it's a real flying visit, then.'

As the waiter approached with their wine she put down the menu. 'I think I'll go with your suggestion of the clam chowder.'

Cal placed their orders and then lifted up his glass. 'So, what shall we drink to?' he asked.

She met his eyes across the table and felt an immediate rush of adrenalin inside. How was he able to do that to her? she wondered. He only had to look at her a certain way and she felt like melting.

'How about, being out and not surrounded by a camera crew for the first time in weeks?' she said lightly.

He smiled. 'I'll definitely drink to that.'

'There's a great view from here, isn't there?' she said, turning her attention away from him to the window, trying hard to fight the feeling of intimacy that had suddenly sprung up between them from nowhere.

'Yes, a great view.'

She was aware that his gaze hadn't followed hers towards the bay, and that he was still looking at her. What was he thinking? she wondered.

She watched a passenger boat heading out for Alcatraz, cutting across the blue of the water, leaving a white froth in its wake.

'What did you do with your wedding and engagement ring?' Cal asked her suddenly.

She turned to look at him, the question taking her completely by surprise. 'They are in a jewellery box at my parents' house.'

'So you didn't think of throwing them out?'

'No.' There was silence as she met the blue of his eyes. Then she looked away, feeling uncomfortable. She didn't want him to think she was a sentimental fool. 'They were too good to just throw away...too pretty...I did think of selling them once...but I just didn't get around to it.'

'Was that when you were having problems with Chandler?'

'Probably...' She shrugged. 'I can't remember. To be honest, Cal, some of that time just after you left is a bit of a blur now.'

The waiter brought their food and they fell silent for a while.

'I meant it when I said I'd help you out with this Chandler business,' Cal said when they were left alone again.

'I know you did.' She glanced back at him and smiled. 'And thanks for not saying "I told you so".'

'You're not the first artist to have been taken to the cleaners, Kirsten. And, if it makes you feel better, I wasn't thinking clearly after Bethany died either. Something like that alters all your perceptions. It's a wonder you were able to think about work at all.'

'If I hadn't I would have gone completely off the rails. I needed something to focus on.' It was strange how she could bear for him to talk about Bethany now. Only a few short weeks ago she would have panicked if he had as much as mentioned her name.

'It's not too late to get my lawyers on to Chandler. We might not recover much of the money but you'd get some satisfaction.'

Kirsten shook her head. 'I've wasted enough money on lawyers. I think it's better just to learn my lesson and forget about it.'

'I hate the thought of that weasel getting off, though,' Cal muttered angrily.

'So do I.' She smiled at him. 'But there's nothing we can do now. Thanks for the offer of support, though, Cal. It does mean a lot.'

'Better late than never?' Cal said drily. 'Maybe if I'd hung around for a while longer after Bethany you wouldn't have got in with Chandler in the first place.'

'And maybe I would.' She looked across at him sharply. 'You can't say that, Cal. I've always been a woman who makes up her own mind...remember?'

'Yeah...I remember.' He grinned.

'Anyway, it's turned out OK in the end. Because of Chandler I had to give up my music. And, although I was extremely upset at the time, acting has turned out to be a positive experience for me.'

'I wondered why you'd given up on your singing career.'

'Chandler had me signed so tightly into an impossible contract that in the end it was easier to just walk away and wait for the time limit on it to expire.'

'That must have hurt? You loved your music so much.' She nodded. 'It wasn't easy.'

'But you rose to the challenge of acting very well. I was very proud of you when I read all those wonderful reviews about your performance on Broadway.'

'Were you?' She smiled.

'I think it was that performance that got you the part in his film,' Cal reflected.

'How do you know that?'

Cal shrugged. 'I heard a whisper.'

'Well, I'm glad to have this part; for one thing, it will be the best money I've earned in a long time. Broadway earned me a great reputation but little else.'

'What will you do when the film is finished?' Cal asked.

'I'd like to go back to my music. It's still my first love,' she admitted cautiously. 'And I'll be free of Chandler's contract at the end of the year.'

'I heard you playing the piano at your parents; it was as magical as ever.' He glanced over at her. 'And maybe getting out of acting is not a bad decision. I know how it can suck you up and tear you apart if you're not careful.'

'Is that really how you feel about the profession?' She frowned. 'I thought you loved it.'

'I've made a good living out of it.' Cal shrugged. 'But it's a fickle paymaster, and a false way of life.'

The waiter brought their main course and the conversation drifted to Kirsten's music.

Cal suggested that she make a re-recording of one of her old songs for a new album.

Kirsten reached for her wine and listened as he talked. For a while it was as if the years had rolled back, and she remembered how exciting and stimulating she had always found Cal's company.

She remembered how ideas had always sparkled when she was in his company; how they had laughed and argued but always gelled together somehow, heightening creativity along the way.

They ordered a cappuccino after their meal and then, as if they were both loath to break the sudden repartee between them, ordered a refill.

We were so good together, Kirsten thought suddenly. Where did all that go…how did we end up so far apart. She looked across at him and felt an overwhelming sadness for what had been lost. I want him back, she thought fiercely. I want to go back to what we once shared.

'Cal…Cal McCormick?' A deep, booming male voice interrupted them and they broke apart from the depths of their conversation and looked up as a portly middle-aged man walked across towards them. 'Thought it was you.'

'Hello, Berni.' Cal stood up and shook hands with th

man as he stopped by their table. 'This is a pleasant surprise.'

'Well, I've got the advantage over you there. I knew you were in town. Maeve told me she saw you last night.'

'That's right.'

Kirsten felt her heart plunge somewhere down towards her toes. Hearing Berni confirm her suspicions about where Cal had been last night was not surprising, yet it hurt. She felt as if reality had just marched in and slapped her forcibly across the face.

'Maeve's here with me now,' Berni continued jovially. 'Outside parking the car, in fact; she'll be up in a minute.'

Kirsten's temperature seemed to shoot up. A reunion with Maeve was definitely not welcome.

'I believe you're filming in town?' Berni slanted a curious look at Kirsten and she forced herself to smile.

'Yes, this is my co-star, Kirsten Brindle. Kirsten, this is Berni Goldstein—we worked together on that film in London.' Cal made the introductions smoothly. 'Berni was the assistant director.'

'Pleased to meet you.' Kirsten smiled.

'Likewise,' Berni said, shaking her hand.

'So, what's this whisper Maeve's been telling me about our new business venture?' Berni asked, turning his attention back to Cal.

'That's not up for discussion yet, Berni.' There was a steely note in Cal's voice that Kirsten recognised straight away as one not to argue with.

Obviously Berni did too, because he immediately backtracked and tapped the side of his nose. 'Know what you mean, Cal,' he said, his voice lowering into agreement and collusion.

What was that about? Kirsten wondered. She didn't have time to think about it, however, because Maeve came into the restaurant at that moment.

'Darling!' Her eyes lit up as she saw Cal across the room. 'What a lovely surprise!'

She hadn't changed a bit, Kirsten thought as she watched her walk towards them. She had a fabulous figure, slender, yet very voluptuous, and the bright red dress she was wearing emphasised every curve. Her hair was dark and straight and it swung with a gleam of health as she reached to embrace Cal as if she hadn't seen him in years.

'You didn't tell me last night that you were coming out for lunch,' she said, a note of rebuke in her husky tone. 'We could have arranged a foursome.' Her gaze travelled to Kirsten and her eyes widened. 'Kirsten…honey! My goodness, this is a blast from the past. It's ages since I saw you.'

Kirsten forced herself to smile. 'Hello, Maeve. Brian not with you?'

'No. He's flying in tomorrow for a business meeting with Berni. I've come on ahead of him to get some uninterrupted shopping done, and attend to a few personal matters.'

'Well, it's good to shop without the men being around,' Kirsten agreed, trying hard to get rid of the cynicism in her voice. Shopping indeed, she thought derisively. Spending a couple of nights with Cal was more like it.

'So, how are you, Kirsten?' Maeve continued in a softer tone, a look of sympathy in her dark eyes.

'I'm fine, thank you, Maeve,' Kirsten said firmly.

'Good. Cal's been telling me all about this film that you're making together. It sounds wonderful, you must be so thrilled to get such a good part.'

'Well, I'm enjoying working with Cal.' Kirsten smiled, hoping that would irritate her.

'Cal's wonderful, isn't he?' Maeve gushed. 'One of the kindest people I know.'

'OK, Maeve, don't overdo it,' Cal said drily.

'Sorry, darling, I'm embarrassing you now.' Mae

smiled at him warmly. 'We'll go and leave you to enjoy the rest of your lunch.'

'OK, see you later,' Cal said easily.

'Yes, see you later, darling.' Maeve reached over and kissed him on the cheek again.

'Give me a ring, will you, Cal?' Berni said before he started to follow Maeve away to their table. 'I'd like to discuss that other business with you.' He tapped his nose again.

'OK; are you at the Excellency Hotel, same as Maeve?'

'Yeah...I'll be there for three more days.' Berni smiled at Kirsten. 'Nice meeting you, Kirsten,' he said. 'Enjoy the rest of your lunch.'

'Sorry about that,' Cal muttered as he sat back down at the table.

'What was all that ''other business'' about?' Kirsten asked, tapping her nose in a mocking parody of the other man.

Cal stared at her distractedly for a moment then shook his head. 'Oh, it was nothing.'

'It didn't sound like nothing.'

'I'll tell you later.'

In other words, he didn't want to talk to her about it either, Kirsten thought. But, whatever it was, he'd obviously discussed it with Maeve.

Kirsten felt the surreal bubble that had surrounded them during their meal burst into reality, dragging her forcibly from the past and what they had once shared back to the present. There was no point wishing for Cal back. You couldn't go back in time, no matter how much you wanted to.

She heard the other woman's laughter floating across the restaurant and glanced over, noting the fact that three waiters were hovering in attendance around her.

'Would you like another coffee?' Cal asked as the waiter cleared their dishes away.

She shook her head and looked at her watch, startled to find it was nearly four. Where had those hours gone? she wondered dazedly.

'I enjoyed what I had, Cal.' She smiled. 'But I'd really like to go now.'

CHAPTER TEN

THEY were in the car heading back to the house when Kirsten's mobile phone rang.

It was Jason, and Kirsten couldn't help feeling relieved as his friendly tone cut the tense silence that had suddenly descended since she and Cal had left the restaurant.

'My plane has just landed and I'm heading for my hotel,' he announced cheerfully. 'What time should I pick you up tonight?'

'About seven-thirty, eight o'clock?' Kirsten suggested.

'OK, but Kirsten…?'

'Yes?' She frowned as she heard the hesitation in Jason's tone.

'Do you think we could go somewhere quiet? I've got something I want to talk to you about and I'd rather do it in relative privacy.'

'Oh!' Kirsten felt a jolt of surprise at the request and at the sudden nervousness in her friend's tone. It was unlike Jason; he was usually so confident and gregarious, always suggesting parties and busy, trendy restaurants when they went out. 'Well…hold on a minute.' Kirsten covered the mouthpiece of her phone and looked over at Cal. 'You are going out tonight, Cal, aren't you?' she asked, remembering that he had told Maeve he'd see her later.

'Why?' Cal took his eyes off the road and glanced at her.

'I thought I'd cook dinner for Jason at the house.'

'I see.' Cal transferred his attention back to the road. 'Fine, go ahead.' He shrugged.

'Thanks.' She took her hand away from the phone. 'Come around to the house, Jason, and I'll cook for us.'

155

'Are you sure you don't mind?'

She heard the relief in his voice and smiled. 'No, of course not; a quiet night in will be very pleasant.'

'Is ol' Jason on an economy drive?' Cal asked derisively as she put the phone back in her bag.

'No, he's not,' Kirsten replied, annoyed by his tone. 'There's something he wants to talk to me about in private.'

'Well, if he's going to propose, the least he could do is take you out to a decent restaurant.' Cal shook his head. 'You want to ditch him, Kirsten.'

'Propose?' Kirsten looked across at Cal in surprise. It hadn't occurred to her for one minute that Jason might be working himself up to propose to her! 'I don't think so, Cal. He's probably been working really hard and just needs a quiet night.' Even as she said the words, she could hear the uncertainty in her own voice.

Cal could hear it too. He pulled the car to a standstill outside the house and turned to look at her. 'I know you don't want to hear this from me, Kirsten, but that guy is not right for you.'

'You're right.' Kirsten turned and reached for the door handle. 'I don't want to hear it from you.'

She marched up to the front door, her heart thundering with a mixture of apprehension and anger. Cal had no right to talk to her like that about Jason. Of course he wasn't going to propose to her...but even if he did, it was none of Cal's damn business. He had a nerve to preach about suitability when he was still seeing a married woman after all these years!

When Cal followed Kirsten into the house a few minutes later she was in the kitchen, going through the cupboards. 'I'm going to have to go out to the shops to buy a few things,' she said as she noticed him standing in the doorway watching her.

'Are you going to tell Jason about us?'

'Us?' She turned away from the cupboard and flicked a nervous glance over at him.

'Yes, "us"…our night of passion together.' He watched as her face flooded with colour.

'We both agreed that was a mistake, Cal, so why should I mention it to Jason?' Her voice was unsteady.

'What happens if you're pregnant?' he asked, folding his arms across his chest and fixing her with a direct look that was very unnerving.

'I'm not pregnant, Cal.' Her voice trembled slightly.

'You're sure?'

She nodded. 'Yes, I'm sure.' For a second she felt the weight of disappointment that had settled on her last week when she had discovered this. Then she turned away from him and tried to continue with her thoughts about dinner. It was crazy to be disappointed; she should be relieved.

We've had a narrow escape, she told herself briskly, sensibly. Cal didn't love her and it would have been foolish in the extreme to go down the same path with him again.

'I still don't think Jason is the right person for you,' Cal said heavily into the silence.

Was he relieved about her condition…or lack of condition? she wondered. In a way she longed for him to say something more about it…she didn't want to talk about Jason.

'I don't know what makes you think you're qualified to speak about who's right and who's wrong for me,' she snapped.

'Well, I was your husband, Kirsten, even if it was for a short space of time. I think I know you pretty well.'

'You don't know me at all, Cal,' she said shakily, flashing him a furious look.

'I think I know you well enough to discern that you wouldn't have slept with me the other night if you were in love with Jason,' he said quietly.

For a few seconds their eyes met and held. He was right.

she acknowledged, and hated herself for the admission. Was she really so damn predictable…? Miss Goody Two Shoes—wouldn't two-time a man she loved…and, worse, wouldn't sleep with a man if she didn't love him, unlike wonderfully sophisticated Maeve…

'Well, you're wrong, Cal,' she said furiously, swinging away from him. 'You couldn't be more wrong.'

'I think you fell into Jason's arms on the rebound,' Cal continued in a calm, low tone as if she hadn't spoken.

'What? And I'm still on the rebound from you now after two years?' Her voice was filled with bitter derision. 'My, but you can be arrogant sometimes.'

'You don't love Jason, Kirsten; I don't care what you say to me. He may be a very pleasant guy, but if you say yes to him tonight you'll be making the biggest mistake of your life.'

She swung her head round angrily and looked over at him. 'Just mind your own business, Cal,' she told him firmly. 'If I decide to say yes to Jason, that will be my decision.'

There was silence for a few seconds…

'I still think you should tell him that we slept together a couple of weeks ago. If he's as nice a guy as you say he is maybe he deserves to know the truth.'

'Yes, he's a nice guy, but what happened between us is none of his business.'

'If he's coming around here to ask you to marry him is very much his business. Maybe I should fill him in little.'

Her eyes widened in disbelief. 'You wouldn't?'

Cal shrugged. 'Sometimes us men have to look out for each other, don't we?'

'That's outrageous, Cal! You wouldn't dare!'

Kirsten didn't like the gleam in Cal's eyes. Saying that to him might not have been a good idea. He'd dare anything if the mood struck him, she realised.

The telephone in the hall started to ring but neither of them made any move to answer it.

The answer machine cut in and Theo's voice filled the air. 'Cal, I've tried to ring your mobile but it's switched off. Would you phone me, please? It's urgent.'

Cal turned away from her and marched through to the hall to pick up the phone. Kirsten heard him say a few short words, then the front door closed behind him as he went out.

Kirsten closed her eyes in relief. Don't come back, she wanted to shout after him. But as soon as her anger towards Cal's high-handed attitude had disappeared she started to think about Jason. He wasn't really going to propose to her, was he?

The table in the dining room was laid with a white damask tablecloth. Candlelight flickered over the silver cutlery and the display of pink roses. Soft music filtered out from the stereo in the lounge.

Kirsten stood back and surveyed her handiwork. She had worked very hard to get everything organised, had had to go shopping for a multitude of things and had even tried to be adventurous with the food. A Creole recipe she had found in a book in the store was now simmering heartily in the kitchen. Had she gone a bit overboard with everything? she wondered suddenly. She didn't want to give Jason the wrong idea.

Glancing at her watch, she saw that it was almost half-past seven. He would be here any minute. She walked across to the mirror in the lounge and checked her appearance. Did the black dress dip a little too provocatively at the cleavage? she wondered, adjusting it to try and retain some modesty.

Ordinarily she wouldn't have given a second thought to any of these things. Jason's company was always so relaxing and undemanding, and it was pleasant to put herself out a little for him and cook something. But Cal's assumption that he was going to propose to her had thrown her into a bit of a panic. Cal was way off track, she reassured herself. For a start, his theory that she was involved with Jason on the rebound couldn't be further from the truth.

Jason had been there for her when Cal had left, but only as a friend; there had never been a romance. So why would he be rushing around here now to propose to her? No...Cal definitely had it wrong. Feeling a bit better, she turned away from her reflection.

At least Cal had thought better of his earlier threats and had decided to do the decent thing and stay away, she thought, pouring herself a weak gin and tonic. He was probably with Maeve...maybe even in bed with her, making the most of the time they had left before Brian arrived.

The picture this painted in her mind threw a renewed dart of anger through her body. 'You're better off without him, Kirsten,' she told herself shakily.

A sound in the hallway made her put down her drink and head out to investigate. She half expected it to be Jason knocking on the door; she got a shock when she saw Cal letting himself in the front door.

'What are you doing here?' she asked nervously.

'I live here,' Cal said drily.

'Yes, but I thought you were going out tonight—'

'I am but I've been stuck in a meeting with Theo for the last few hours.' Cal's eyes flicked over her appearance, lingering for a second too long on the heart-shaped neckline. 'Aren't you a bit dressed up for dinner at home?'

'It's just a plain black dress...' She trailed off, wondering what the hell she was doing justifying her appearance to him! 'Look, are you going straight back out? Because—'

'Yeah...don't worry. I'm not going to cramp your style.' He walked past her, his glance taking in the beautifully laid table in the dining room. 'You have been busy.'

'Yes, and Jason's going to be here in a few minutes.'

She followed him through to the lounge. 'Cal, what are you doing?' She watched him as he walked to the glasses and bottles she had left on the sideboard and started to pour himself a whiskey.

'What does it look like I'm doing?' he asked. 'I'm tired and I'm pouring myself a drink.' He reached out and switched off the music on the stereo. 'It's very dark in here, Kirsten. I can't see a thing,' he muttered. 'Put the overhead light on, will you?'

'No, I will not!' She put her hand on her hip and glared at him. 'I'm having a dinner party, Cal. I want the lighting low and I want the music back on.'

'Are you trying to hide something from good ol' Jason?' Cal asked, a mocking gleam of humour in his eyes. 'You know, I read somewhere that most men choose a wife in light so dim that they wouldn't even buy a suit by it.'

Kirsten didn't know what to say to that. 'Is that supposed to be some kind of joke?' she asked unsteadily. 'Because—'

'No, it wasn't a joke. Just a little reassurance.' His voice lowered huskily. 'You don't need the lights down low, Kirsten; you're gorgeous.'

A molten wave of heat stole through her body as she noticed the way he was looking at her. There was something very sexual about that gleam in his eye, something almost primitively dangerous about him as he walked over towards her.

'Jason's going to be here in a minute,' she said again, apprehensively wondering if she should turn and walk away, and yet…she didn't want to. She was held captive by the almost challenging mood of excitement he conjured up in her.

'I know, I heard you.' He stopped a few steps away from her and surveyed her critically. 'You should have stayed in the jeans you were wearing this afternoon. That dress is far too provocative.'

'Cal, I...' Her voice trailed off as she watched him put his glass down on the coffee table.

'In fact, it's far too good to be wasted on a night in with good ol' Jason.'

'I wish you'd stop calling him that.' She took a step backwards as he came closer.

'OK, that dress is far too sexy for any man's peace of mind... There, is that better?' There was a teasing light in his eyes now.

She didn't know how to contend with Cal when he was in this kind of a mood. 'Cal, please...you know I can't deal with this right now...' She took another step backwards and found herself right up against the wall.

'Deal with what?'

'Deal...with the level of...sensuality that you can always...always exert over me...'

'Can I?' He smiled at that. Then his head lowered and he kissed her. This was no gentle, sweet kiss, it was controlling and dominant and it sent Kirsten's senses reeling. It made every nerve in her body react with vibrant, pulsating need. Instinctively she kissed him back, her heart racing, her blood pumping through her veins with a tingling ecstasy. She felt his hands on her body and suddenly she was pressing herself closer, all her self-control of the last few weeks vanishing instantly.

She felt his hands touching her breasts through the fine silk material, and she longed to be free of its constraints...longed to just give herself to him here and now...

The shrill sound of the front doorbell cut into her consciousness. Cal pulled back.

'That's a bit of bad timing, isn't it?' he remarked.

She frowned, wondering how he was able to sound so together, so cool, when she was in a state of chaos inside.

'You shouldn't have done that,' she said unsteadily.

'Maybe not.'

'Why did you?'

His eyes lingered on her lips and she moistened them instinctively. 'I did it to show you how wrong you are if you say yes to Jason. It would be a mistake, Kirsten, and there's been enough of those between us.'

The doorbell rang again.

'I'd better let him in,' Cal said, stepping back from her. 'Give you a chance to pull yourself together.'

'How kind…' she managed sardonically.

He smiled at her. 'And you do look gorgeous,' he said softly. 'So I suggest out of fairness to Jason you blow out those candles and turn up the lights.'

She watched as he walked away. He was so damned arrogant, she thought. Who the heck did he think he was, telling her who was right and who was wrong for her? Cal was wrong about Jason's intentions, but even so she did find her hand sneaking out to turn the light-dimmer switch up ever so slightly.

Then she put up a shaking hand to smooth her hair down as she heard Jason's voice in the hall.

She shouldn't have kissed Cal back like that…she thought angrily. What was wrong with her? Why couldn't she control herself around him when she knew damned well that all she was doing was feeding that damned ego of his? He just had to be right…didn't he? Just breezed in and took what he wanted, making his point without regard to her feelings…

'I didn't realise that you were staying with Kirsten.' Jason's voice cut into her thoughts and she quickly moved to glance at her reflection in the mirror. She looked flushed and her lips were swollen!

Hurriedly she put the back of her hand against them in a vain attempt to cool herself again.

'Hi, Kirsten.' Jason stepped into the room just as she moved over to go and welcome him.

He was carrying an enormous bouquet of flowers, which he was half-hidden behind. 'Goodness, what lovely flowers.' She took them from him and leaned to kiss him on the cheek. 'Thanks, Jason, that's so sweet of you.'

Over his shoulder she saw Cal lounging against the door-frame, watching, a cynical light in his blue eyes.

Hastily she pulled her eyes away from his. 'Aren't you going out, Cal?' she asked stiffly as she went to put the flowers on the table in the window.

'I'm going up for a shower first.' Contrary to his words, Cal walked further into the room. 'Can I get you a drink, Jason?' he asked jovially.

'Thanks, I'll have a white wine.'

If Jason thought it was strange that Cal was here playing host, he didn't show it. 'Lovely house, Kirsten, the studio is looking after you well.'

'Well, that's a big bone of contention at the moment,' Kirsten muttered as she watched Cal handing Jason his drink.

'Why's that?'

'I'll tell you later,' Kirsten said, looking pointedly at Cal.

'How was your flight, Jason?' Cal asked, totally ignoring her.

She listened as the two men chatted easily. Jason looked very smart in a dark suit and a pale green shirt. He was very good-looking, she thought, and yet, next to Cal, who was wearing jeans and his blue denim shirt, there was something almost dapper about Jason's appearance.

'It shouldn't have taken that long for us to drive here but we stopped off at Kirsten's parents' and they persuaded us to stay overnight,' she heard Cal telling him, and her nerves suddenly twisted in apprehension. What the hell was he playing at? He wasn't really contemplating telling Jason about…about what had happened between them that night was he?

'It was enjoyable, wasn't it, Kirsten?' He glanced over at her coolly and she felt anger prickle through her. How dared he do this? He had no right.

'It was OK. Dad's a lot better now, Jason,' she said, trying to turn the subject safely away from whatever direction Cal was thinking of leading it.

'Are you cooking something with fish in it?' Cal cut across her suddenly.

'No.' She looked over at him, perplexed by the swift change of subject.

'Really? I could have sworn something smelt a bit fishy.' Kirsten's eyes narrowed on him.

He met her cool stare with a raised eyebrow and a gleam of amusement. 'Maybe it's burning I can smell,' he suggested.

Horrified, Kirsten put her drink down and with an apologetic glance at Jason rushed towards the kitchen to investigate.

'That got her,' Cal remarked with a smile at Jason. He finished his drink and put the glass down. 'Well, I'd better go and get ready. I'm going to that charity do at the Excellency Hotel.'

'Oh? Yes, I heard about that, there's quite a few celebrities going to be there, I believe.'

'Yes. Maeve talked me into going. But I could have done without it tonight. Why don't you and Kirsten drop down here for a drink later?'

Jason nodded. 'Well…I'll suggest it to Kirsten.'

'Was it burning?' Jason asked Kirsten when she returned to the lounge.

'No, it was fine.' Kirsten glanced around the room. 'Where did Cal go?'

'He said he was getting ready to go out.'

Kirsten nodded. 'Did he say anything else to you while I was out of the room?' she asked curiously.

'Not much…why should he?'

'I just wondered,' Kirsten muttered. 'Dinner is ready, Jason, if you'd like to come through.'

*   *   *

They were halfway through their entrée and Cal still hadn't gone out. Kirsten felt completely on edge, especially when the sound of rock music came blaring down the stairs, interrupting the light classical background music that she was playing.

'Sorry about this, Jason.' She got up to close the door.

'That's OK.' Jason grinned at her and she smiled back at him thankfully. At least Jason was easy-going and didn't seem to care too much about the interruption.

'It must be a bit difficult sharing a house with him,' he said sympathetically.

'Oh, Jason, you have no idea!' She rolled her eyes. 'He's the most…infuriating man.'

'Yeah…good-looking, though, isn't he?' Jason said with a grin.

'I suppose.' Kirsten pushed the food around her plate. It tasted great but she wasn't really hungry. 'If you go for those overwhelmingly masculine types…which I don't.. any more.'

Why was she saying that? she wondered as she remembered the feel of Cal's lips crushing and sensual against hers. Instantly her stomach twisted into tight knots of arousal as it screamed its rejection of her words.

'No?' Jason raised his eyebrow and then leaned across to refill her wine glass. 'Listen, Kirsten, I really appreciate you going to so much trouble for me tonight.'

'It wasn't a lot of trouble.'

'Don't lie, Kirsten, you're terrible at it,' Jason said with a laugh.

'Am I?' She took a hasty sip of her wine and wondered what else he'd detected as a lie. 'Anyway, tell me all about what's been happening in LA.' She smiled at him. 'I want all the gossip, now.'

'In a minute; first there is something I've got to say to you.' Jason's voice was suddenly and unusually nervous.

The music flicked off upstairs and in the silence Kirsten could hear her heart beating.

Please don't let Cal be right. Please don't propose to me, she thought wildly. I don't want to have to hurt you, Jason…I don't want to lose your friendship. But I'm in love with Cal.

'Listen, Kirsten…I…' Jason reached across the table suddenly and caught hold of her hand. 'Hell…I don't know how to say this to you.'

'Then maybe you shouldn't say it,' Kirsten told him gently. 'We're good friends, Jason, and—'

'I have to say it…I've been trying to get the courage up to say it to you for ages.'

Kirsten heard Cal's footsteps upstairs and wondered if he was going to suddenly barge in on them.

'The thing is…'

'Yes?' She watched Jason's face anxiously. She couldn't believe it, Cal had been right. After all this time…Jason was going to propose!

'The thing is, Kirsten, I'm gay.'

'Gay?' Kirsten stared at him in stunned amazement.

He nodded. 'I've kept it a secret because I thought it might damage my career…you know, with getting a lot of macho straight parts and—'

'You're gay?'

He watched her with a worried, rueful frown over his eyes. 'Kirsten, I'm so sorry if I've led you to think…well, anything else. I want you to know that I value your friendship more than anyone's and I hope you can understand and forgive me for not saying anything before now.'

'There's nothing to forgive…' She shook her head. 'But I just didn't realise…'

'Can we still be friends?' She heard the anxious note in his voice and it snapped her out of her stunned state.

'I can't believe you've just asked me that,' she said crossly, and squeezed his hand. 'Nothing has changed. I really value your friendship, Jason. You've helped me through some terrible times. You've been a tower of strength and a wonderful friend. I couldn't bear to lose you…'

'Now you are going to make me cry.' Jason sounded very emotional suddenly. He got up from the table and came around to give her a hug.

And that was how Cal found them a few moments later.

They didn't even realise he had walked into the room until he spoke coolly. 'Didn't mean to interrupt such a touching scene.'

They immediately broke apart.

'I'm going out, Kirsten.' His eyes met hers.

She had barely time to register the fact that he had changed into a dark dinner suit and he looked spectacular.

'See you around, Jason.' With a curt nod in the other man's direction, Cal went out and closed the door behind him.

Jason pulled a face at her. 'Do you think he just got the wrong idea?'

'It doesn't matter what idea he got,' Kirsten said, trying to remain indifferent.

Jason retook his seat at the other side of the table. 'Don't give me that line, Kirsten,' he said briskly. 'Of course you care.'

'We're just sharing the house under sufferance. It's not what it seems.' She looked over and met Jason's eyes. He was grinning at her as if she had said something hysterically funny.

'Kirsten, you couldn't be more in love with that guy i you had a sign painted on your back. Which, incidentally…reminds me. Your zip is halfway down at the back of your dress.'

Kirsten felt her face flood with colour.

'Interrupted something, did I?' Jason lifted his glass i a mocking salute.

'Let's not talk about Cal,' she muttered, instinctively withdrawing from the arena. 'Let's talk about you.'

'Yes…but later.' Jason laughed, his usual good humour returning. 'First I've got something to tell you about Cal. Some really juicy gossip.'

'What?'

Jason smiled and looked as if he was thoroughly enjoying himself. 'You know that company that you were asking me about—Sugar Productions?'

'Yes. They're making our film.'

'It belongs to Cal McCormick.'

Kirsten stared at him. 'No.' She shook her head. 'You've got that wrong. Cal is working for them, same as me. We were talking about it this morning. He's going to try and put a word in to get me moved into another house…' Kirsten trailed away as she watched Jason shaking his head.

'Cal is Sugar Productions…take it from me, Kirsten. The secret came out last week and now it's all over Hollywood.'

'But if Cal owns the production company…' Kirsten frowned. 'That would mean he's in charge of everything… That would mean…' Her voice trailed off as horrible realisation dawned. 'That would mean that his influence got me the part in this film…' Her eyes widened with horror. 'And he's chosen to work opposite me. Why would he do that…?' Her mind started to race.

'Because he wants you back,' Jason said with a grin.

Kirsten shook her head. 'Because he feels sorry for me.' Her voice was laced with fury. Suddenly she was remembering Berni and Maeve at the restaurant. Berni had nearly let the secret out and Cal hadn't been at all happy. And what was it Maeve had said…? 'You must be so pleased to get such a good part…Cal's so kind…the kindest person I know.'

The memory made her very uncomfortable. 'I think Cal knew about Chandler all along,' she said slowly now. 'He knew I was ripped off and he got all protective. This is his way of compensating me for the money I lost.'

'You're right. Cal does know about Chandler. I told him ages ago, but—'

'You did what?' Kirsten got up from the table. 'That lying, conniving…!' Kirsten shook her head. 'He was being all sympathetic and innocent about it this morning, pretending he didn't know…trying to draw me out.'

'Well, he probably felt badly about it for you…but as for it being the reason he's doing the film…then I don't think so, Kirsten. Because that's one expensive trip.'

'He's got enough money not to care.' Kirsten's eyes prickled with tears.

'Nobody has that much money!'

Kirsten shook her head. 'I'm so confused, Jason. I thought I got this part off my own bat. I thought I'd done it myself…crikey, I went for enough auditions! To find out it might be Cal's sympathy vote that's landed me it makes my blood boil. I'd rather be poverty-stricken than accept a part under those terms. He's turned me into a laughing stock!'

'Oh, come on, Kirsten! Cal is a businessman at the end of the day. The reason you got the part is that you're one damn fine actress.'

'But how can I be sure of that now?' Kirsten rounded angrily to look at him. 'Well, there's no way I'm continuing with this part. He can litigate if he wants, but I'm out of here.'

Jason frowned. 'I think you're jumping the gun. I met Jack Boyd last week. He was originally signed up for the part Cal took.'

'No, he wasn't. They never got around to signing him…'

'Ah…but they did sign him,' Jason contradicted her. 'He told me himself. The deal was through Gold-Start origi nally. They signed Jack Boyd and you. Then Cal came along and optioned the movie off them. Paid a lot of money out to Jack.'

Kirsten sat back down at the table. 'So he didn't arrange my part in the movie?'

Jason shook his head. 'No. You got that yourself. It was Cal's part in the movie that was acquired…shall we say, covertly?'

'But Cal doesn't need to buy himself parts—Hollywood is screaming out for him.' Kirsten met Jason's eyes across the table. 'What's he playing at?'

'Being near to you?'

Kirsten's heart thumped unsteadily against her chest. She really wanted to believe that. 'But he's still seeing Maeve.'

'Well, you've got me there.' Jason shrugged and leaned back in his chair. 'Maybe he's in love with both of you?'

'Then maybe it's time he made up his mind which one of us he wants.'

Jason looked over at her and smiled. 'That sounds like fighting talk.'

She smiled back. 'Do you know, Jason, I think you're right?'

'He's at the Excellency Hotel with her,' Jason supplied promptly. 'Some kind of charity party, I believe. Shall we go over there and see what's going on?'

Kirsten nodded. 'I think it's about time I did.'

Jason grinned. 'You go for it. But if you don't mind I won't stay around there long…I've got a date later.'

'Oh?'

'His name is Jo and it's pretty serious, Kirsten…hell, it feels good to be able to say that.'

Kirsten smiled at him. 'I'm so pleased for you, Jason,' she said sincerely. 'And I wish you all the happiness in the world.'

CHAPTER ELEVEN

THE massive ballroom was packed with people. Sequinned clothing and jewels sparkled in the mirror-ball light and a band was playing a medley of swing numbers at the far end of the room.

'Maybe we won't be able to find Cal amongst all these people?' Jason had to practically shout to make himself heard.

'If he's here I'll find him,' Kirsten said determinedly. Her eyes moved along the bar and then towards the dance floor, searching for Cal and Maeve amongst the couples. But the floor was so tightly packed it was hard to see the centre.

Then the band struck up a slower, more romantic melody, and as the couples changed and moved she caught a glimpse of Cal at the far side of the floor, talking to Maeve.

'There he is.' Kirsten nudged Jason and he followed the direction of her eyes.

'Right, come on.' Jason took hold of her hand and together they shouldered their way through the crowds.

Maeve was the first to notice them; she smiled coolly. Then Cal turned and met her eyes.

Now that she was here she didn't know what she was going to say to him. All the confident fighting talk that she had been giving Jason on the way over here seemed to evaporate as she looked into his blue eyes.

'We didn't think we'd see you here tonight,' Maeve said

'Spur-of-the-moment decision.' Jason grinned.

Kirsten looked up at Cal again. He didn't say anything and she felt her heart thudding against her chest. Vaguely she was aware of Jason moving closer to Maeve, distracting her, then laughing with her about something. It made the silence between her and Cal seem even more strained.

Cal was the first to speak. 'So, what was your answer?'

'To what?'

'Don't be obtuse, Kirsten,' Cal muttered angrily. 'You know damn well I'm referring to Jason's proposal.'

Out of the corner of Kirsten's eye she saw Jason and Maeve heading off towards the dance floor.

'He didn't ask me.'

Cal frowned as if he hadn't heard her correctly, and with all the noise that surrounded them maybe he hadn't.

'However, he did tell me about Sugar Productions.' Kirsten stepped closer to him.

'What about Sugar Productions?'

'Don't give me that innocent look, Cal McCormick. You lied to me.' She glared at him. 'You own the company.' She reached out and poked him in the chest with one accusing finger. 'All that stuff this morning about knowing people up there...it was all a load of rubbish. You know everyone up there because you've been pulling the strings all along.'

'Have I?'

'You know damn well you have.'

He smiled; it was that teasing smile that she knew so well and it threatened her composure.

She took a deep breath. 'So, what's going on?'

Cal ignored the question. 'What's going on with you and Jason?' he asked instead.

'I'm asking the questions,' Kirsten told him firmly. 'I asked you first.'

Cal smiled ruefully at her. 'You drive a very hard bargain, Kirsten Brindle-McCormick.'

Someone bumped into her and Cal reached out, pulling her closer to him. 'Come on,' he said firmly. 'Let's get out of here.'

Kirsten didn't argue, she allowed him to lead her through

the crowds and down towards the main foyer. But when they were outside he didn't stop, he held her hand and led her across the road towards the quietness of the marina.

'That's better.' He turned and looked at her once they were down by the quay. 'I couldn't hear myself think in there.'

'So, what's going on?' She looked up into his eyes and felt herself shiver with emotion.

'Did you say that Jason didn't propose to you tonight?' he asked with annoying determination.

'Yes…but—'

'The guy must be crazy… You know, it took all my will-power not to drag him physically away from you tonight.'

'Cal! What is going on?' she asked him again. 'Why have you bought that production company? Why did you pay Jack Boyd vast sums of money to get his part?'

Cal didn't answer her immediately; he let his eyes travel over her face, lit by the softness of the moonlight.

'Because it was opposite you…because it was the only way I thought I could get you to start talking to me again…and because I love you, Kirsten, and I want you back.'

Kirsten's heart missed several beats. 'And what about Maeve?' she whispered unsteadily. 'How does she fit into all this—how do you feel about her?'

'Maeve?' Cal frowned. 'Maeve doesn't fit into it any where.'

'Oh, come on, Cal, don't lie to me.' Her eyes shimmered 'I saw you together, you know…that night just after Bethany died.'

Cal frowned. 'Kirsten, I don't know what you're talkin about.'

'That night…' A shiver ran through her voice. 'Whe you took her into your arms and told her you wanted to b with her…I was there. I was watching you from the doo way.'

'Before she went to London, you mean?'

Kirsten nodded. 'You were in the lounge of our house telling her that the only reason you were staying with me was because I had been going through a bad time.'

'I didn't say that!'

'Yes, you did. I heard you.' Kirsten took a deep breath and stepped back from him. 'You were having an affair with her, weren't you?'

Cal shook his head. 'Before we were together I had an affair with Maeve. But it ended a long time ago, Kirsten…we're just friends now.'

'Friends who go to bed together whenever the opportunity presents itself.' Her voice trembled alarmingly. 'Friends who share secrets and whisper together on the phone.'

'What secrets?'

'She knows about you owning the production company…her friend made that clear this afternoon—'

'Kirsten, half of Hollywood knows I own that production company now. Theo spilled the secret a few days ago. That's why he rang this afternoon, to tell me the news was well and truly out there.'

'And where did you spend last night?'

Cal reached across and took hold of her hand. His skin was warm against the coldness of hers. He led her a few steps further down the deserted quay and then stopped. 'I was here.'

She followed his gaze towards the yacht that lay moored beside them, a huge vessel that was just a shadowy shape against the silver moonlit sky. 'And before you ask…I was on my own.'

When she didn't say anything he continued softly, 'I stayed here because I wanted to make love to my wife but she was sleeping across the corridor from me…and I was unsure if my self-control would hold for another night…'

'Cal…' Her voice broke suddenly. 'Don't lie to me. I'd rather know the truth and deal with it—'

He pulled her closer and held her tightly against his chest for a while. 'This is the truth, Kirsten. OK, I haven't been living life as a monk since our divorce. I've played around…I've made mistakes…hell, Kirsten, I wasn't thinking straight either after Bethany died.'

'I know.' She squeezed her eyes tightly closed as she leaned against him.

'But my affair with Maeve ended three months before she married Brian and long before I met you. Yes, we're still friends, but my feelings for her are sympathetic, not sexual. She's had a tough life and—'

'Oh, heavens, Cal, don't start with the sympathy on Maeve.' Kirsten pulled away from him and wiped the tears from her eyes fiercely. 'I can't stick it when you start to stand up for her.'

'She did have a rough childhood. Like me, her parents died when she was young but she wasn't as lucky as I was. She was packed off to a home where…well, let's just say, if she's a bit emotionally unstable somehow…she's got just cause.'

'And did she have just cause to tell me when I was pregnant that she was your first love?' Kirsten asked angrily. 'She made it very clear to me how much you thought of her…and how you had only married me because I was pregnant.'

'What? How dare she say something so outrageous? It's a downright lie!'

She heard the shock in Cal's voice and continued fiercely, 'And you were in each other's arms that day…you were telling her how much you wanted to be with her.'

'She was crying, Kirsten…I was just comforting her. thought she was a friend.' Anger laced through Cal' words. 'How wrong could I be? I can hardly believe tha she told such a vicious downright lie to you.'

'Well, she did.'

'I know she's emotionally unstable, Kirsten...but I never dreamt she would say something so terrible. You do believe me when I say it's not true...don't you?' He looked at her anxiously. 'That night when you saw us together in the lounge—she was upset when I told her I wasn't going to London. She was apprehensive about making the commitment to the movie on her own.' Cal frowned. 'A few weeks before that she had tried to commit suicide.' He saw the surprise on Kirsten's face and grimaced. 'She asked me not to tell anyone about that and I respected the confidence out of pity for her. But I realise now what a mistake that was... I should have told you. It's just that you were so low yourself and it was just a dreadful time—'

'Why did she try to commit suicide?'

'She was very troubled in her marriage to Brian and there were problems from her childhood that were still haunting her. She came around that night needing moral support and I was worried about her state of mind, so I tried to give her that support as a friend...nothing more.'

Kirsten was totally stunned. 'I had no idea she suffered from depression.'

'She's been in therapy for two years, but she's a lot better now, mostly down to the fact that she has a new man in her life. Berni has helped her tremendously.'

'Berni!'

Cal nodded. 'She's going to leave Brian for him.'

'Cal, I thought you were in love with her! That she was the reason you were so fired up about taking that part in London.' Kirsten shook her head.

'I wanted to go to London and make the movie because I knew it would be my biggest chance of success... You know that. I told you that. But I didn't want to go because Maeve was there—'

'That's what it sounded like that night.'

'Well, despite what it sounded like...Maeve was never

a deciding factor in why I wanted to go to London...
never...' His voice was emphatic. 'If you want we can go
across and confront Maeve with this now. In fact, I
wouldn't mind asking her what the hell she was playing at,
telling you such a pack of lies.' Cal sounded absolutely
furious.

Kirsten shook her head. 'I think under the circumstances
we should leave the episode alone, Cal,' she said shakily.

'Suggesting that I married you because you were pregnant is inexcusable. I married you, Kirsten, because I love
you, and she knows that.'

The sincerity in Cal's voice made Kirsten catch her
breath. She looked down at her hands. 'Maybe it was just
the timing of everything that was bad. Seeing you with
Maeve in your arms was the last straw. I was hurting so
much. I felt as if I was to blame for Bethany's death...as
pathetic as it sounds, I needed you to tell me you loved
me.'

'I did tell you...'

Kirsten shook her head. 'I was thinking...you know
when we were in the kitchen at Mum and Dad's.
Remembering the last time you told me you loved me. It
was before Bethany died...' She looked up at him then and
tears started to fall down her cheeks. 'After Bethany you
never said those words to me...'

She didn't realise how hard she was crying until Cal
pulled her into his arms and just held her.

'I'm sorry...' He whispered the words huskily against
her ear. 'I'm so...so sorry, Kirsten. I was trying to be so
strong and together...but I was too busy blaming myself.'

They stood there a long time, wrapped in each other's
arms. Kirsten didn't want to let go of him, didn't want to
move. The breeze whipped up and whistled musically in
the rigging of the yachts in the marina. That and the sound
of the tide gently lapping against the side of the quay was
all that filled her senses for a while.

Cal was the one to pull away. 'Come on, let's go on board,' he suggested gently.

Silently she slipped off her high heels and followed him up the gangplank and across the rope-strewn deck.

Cal switched on a lamp in the main cabin below the wheelhouse, illuminating the white settees, the polished wooden floors and brass fitments. 'How long have you had this yacht?'

'Six months. I bought her in England and sailed back on her once the film was finished. It did me a lot of good being on my own for a while. Gave me time to think and plan…'

'Is that when you got the idea to set up a production company?'

'Amongst other things.'

He watched as she dabbed at her eyes with a tissue. 'Kirsten, will you ever forgive me for the mess I've made of things?' he asked softly. 'I should never have left you and gone to England.'

'I told you to go.' She shrugged.

'But I should have stayed near by and tried to work things out. When I got to England I realised I'd made a mistake and I wanted to come back, but I was tied into a contract and I couldn't get out of it.' Cal looked over at her bleakly. 'All I could think about was that you were with Jason and I'd blown it.'

She smiled at that. 'There was never anything between me and Jason.'

'Now, come on, Kirsten—'

'He's gay, Cal,' she told him, and watched his look of surprised incredulity with a certain amount of satisfaction. At least she wasn't the only one who hadn't realised, she thought wryly. 'That's one of Hollywood's better kept secrets, isn't it…?' she said lightly. 'Don't tell anyone, Cal. I don't think Jason is ready to go public with it.'

'Of course I won't tell anyone…' Cal shook his head. 'So there was never any romance between you?'

'We're just friends…'

'I really thought—'

'And I really thought that you and Maeve were having an affair,' she cut across him.

Cal came across to her then, an intense look of seriousness in his eyes. 'You do believe me, Kirsten, when I say there's nothing between us?'

'I believe you,' she whispered softly.

Cal took both of her hands in his. 'I hope so, because from the day I first met you there has never been a place in my heart for any other woman. I know I didn't deal with things right when Bethany died—'

'Neither of us did,' she whispered. 'We both wanted her so much…and in the end we allowed that grief to cloud all our judgements. We pushed each other away at a time when we should have been clinging to each other. Nothing seemed as if it would ever be right again.'

'I want to make it right again,' Cal said. 'I want you so much, Kirsten… I love you so much…'

She flung herself into his arms. 'I can hardly believe you're saying this to me, Cal… I've longed to hear those words for so long. I love you so much.'

He bent and kissed her and it was a long time before either of them spoke again, as passion flowed with uninhibited strength between them.

'Say it again,' he murmured huskily as he pulled back.

'Which bit?' She moved closer.

'The bit where you tell me you love me. I'm afraid might be dreaming.'

'I love you, Cal… I've always loved you.' She peppered her words with kisses. 'And I want you back. I want—'

Cal suddenly swung her up off her feet, cutting her sentence off in mid-flow. 'And I want to take you to bed. Right now,' he growled huskily.

They undressed each other with impatient need as soo

as they reached the cabin, caressing each other and kissing
with heated desire.

It was much later, as they lay sated and exhausted in
each other's arms in the huge double bed, that Kirsten's
mind drifted back over their lovemaking and then to their
previous conversation.

'What will you do now?' she asked sleepily, half to herself.

'Get my breath back and make love to you again.'

Kirsten smiled. 'I was thinking about the fact that you
own that production company. I can still hardly believe it.
What were your intentions?'

'For a start, I'm going to give up acting.'

'Really?' She was startled by this. 'Why?'

'I could never say that it was a burning ambition. I fell
into it, and I've decided it's time I fell out of it again. I'm
going to concentrate on my writing and on the production
side of things.'

'Just like that?'

'I've made a lot of money, so I can't complain about
acting. But it's a fickle career; one day you're up, the next
you're down. To say nothing of the fact that it plays hell
with your love-life.'

She sat up slightly. 'Which reminds me. Did I get the
part in this film because of your influence—?'

'No, you did not.' Cal frowned. 'You got that yourself;
the film was cast before I took things over. It was my part
that I engineered.'

'And what about all that business about us having to be
seen together for PR?'

'What about it…?'

'Was that your idea or the studio's?'

'Mine.' He grinned at her and kissed her lips. 'Pretty
good, wasn't it?'

'And that morning when you dashed around to my apartment and told me Theo was annoyed because I wasn't flying to San Francisco—'

'Theo couldn't have cared less. But it was a great opportunity for me to be with you for the drive down. I also phoned your parents just to enlist a bit of support—'

Kirsten sat up completely now, and looked down at him in mock-fury. 'Phoning my parents was going too far, Cal—'

'Desperate measures called for some very determined action.' He smiled sleepily. 'And it was well worth it, I have to say now…'

'Cal McCormick, I don't know whether to kiss or kill you,' she sighed happily.

'Then marry me,' he said seriously, sitting up and breaking the playful mood.

'Are you serious?' She frowned suddenly.

'Of course I'm serious; I've never been more serious.'

She felt her heart drumming against her chest.

'Let's run away together…or sail away together and get married as soon as possible,' he said firmly. 'We could go to a Caribbean island if you'd like, or—'

'Cal. I can't do that.' She cut across him briskly.

'I see.' He stared at her. 'Do you mind telling me why not?'

'Because…' she smiled at him '…you promised your aunt in London that she could come to the wedding…and I need time to get ready and—'

Whatever else she was going to say was cut off as Cal pounced on her, making her squeal as he pulled her down and pinned her firmly to the bed.

'Repeat after me,' he said firmly. 'Yes, Cal, I will marry you, and we will live happily ever after.'

'Yes, Cal, I will marry you—and—'

The rest of her words were drowned out by his kisses and the passion of their embrace.

EPILOGUE

KIRSTEN woke in the cool light of morning. She felt oddly disorientated, as if she were still asleep and dreaming.

She reached out a hand to the space next to her, but Cal had gone.

The shrill sound of a baby's cry filled the air and sleepily Kirsten pushed the covers back and picked up her dressing gown.

The nursery at the front of the house was painted yellow and it seemed filled with golden sunlight. Kirsten went across to the cot and looked inside at the four-month-old baby.

As soon as Pippa saw her mother the tears stopped. The cute little legs in the pale yellow sleepsuit kicked and she laughed and gurgled, plump little arms outstretched as she waited to be lifted from her cot.

'What was all that noise about?' Kirsten asked, smiling. 'What were all those crocodile tears about?' She reached out and touched the tiny fingers, gently holding them as she looked into her daughter's eyes, so big and blue, just like Cal's.

'What a big noise for a little girl,' she said teasingly, and then lifted her out to hold her in her arms.

The door opened behind her and Cal came in. 'What's all the commotion about?' he asked with a grin.

'I think she knows it's her big day today.' Kirsten said, and turned her attention back to the baby. 'You know something exciting is going to happen today, don't you, darling? Today you're going to be christened—Philippa Jordana McCormick.'

183

'It has a good ring to it, doesn't it?' Cal said, reaching to kiss the top of the baby's head.

'A very good ring.' Kirsten smiled at her husband. 'Happy anniversary, by the way.'

'Happy anniversary.' Cal reached across and kissed her, and for a while the three of them were held close. 'Who would believe that it's two years today since we got married again?'

'The happiest two years of my life,' Kirsten whispered tremulously. 'Thank you, Cal.'

Pippa gurgled and wriggled between them impatiently. 'I think she's trying to tell us that we don't have time for this,' Kirsten laughed as she pulled away from him. 'And she's right. Mum and Dad will be here soon and I've got a million and one things to do.'

'Well, they can all wait,' Cal said firmly as he took his daughter from her arms. 'Because your present is downstairs and I've gone to such a lot of trouble to get it here without you knowing that everything else is going to have to wait.'

'What is it…?' Intrigued, Kirsten followed him out into the corridor and down the elegant curving staircase. They watched as he opened the front door.

A brand-new shiny red car sat on the drive.

Kirsten looked at it in stunned amazement.

'It's an automatic,' Cal said with a grin. 'If you're going to drive to the church I can't stand one more crunch of those gears in that old jalopy.'

Modern Romance™
...seduction and
passion guaranteed

Tender Romance™
...love affairs that
last a lifetime

Sensual Romance™
...sassy, sexy and
seductive

Blaze™
...sultry days and
steamy nights

Medical Romance™
...medical drama on
the pulse

Historical Romance™
...rich, vivid and
passionate

29 new titles every month.

*With all kinds of Romance for
every kind of mood...*

MILLS & BOON®

Makes any time special™

MAT4

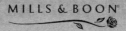

Modern Romance™

WOLFE'S TEMPTRESS by Robyn Donald

Rowan was charming, with an irresistible beauty and an innocence that took Wolfe Talamantes by surprise. The combination was beguiling, and they fell into bed at first sight. Then Rowan fled. But Wolfe had found her once – he'd find her again…

A SHOCKING PASSION by Amanda Browning

Good looks and sophisticated charm have always been Ellie's downfall, and the moment she sets eyes on the irresistible Jack Thornton all reason disappears! Jack is set on skilful seduction and Ellie is determined to resist. But one taste of intoxicating passion and she knows she wants more…

THE BILLIONAIRE IS BACK by Myrna Mackenzie

After convincing herself that she doesn't need a man in her life, Helena meets Jackson Castle. The attraction is instantaneous, but Helena's conspicuous pregnancy is a constant reminder that passion has a price…

THE MILLIONAIRE'S WAITRESS WIFE by Carolyn Zane

Millionaire Dakota Brubaker found it refreshing that his sassy waitress mistook him for a regular guy. But just as he was about to ask Elizabeth out, she proposed to him! She urgently needed a working class groom to shock her interfering family. Could Dakota keep his millions secret?

On sale 5th April 2002

Available at most branches of WH Smith, Tesco, Martins, Borders, Eason, Sainsbury's and most good paperback bookshops.

0302/01b

Treat yourself this Mother's Day to the ultimate indulgence

3 brand new romance novels and a box of chocolates

= only £7.99

Available from 15th February

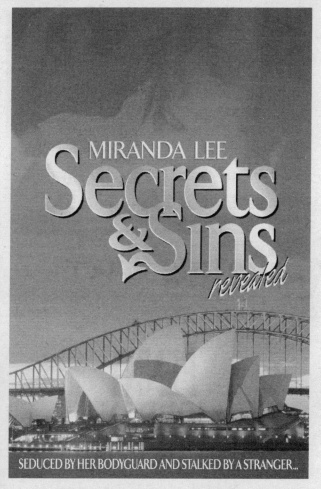

SEDUCED BY HER BODYGUARD AND STALKED BY A STRANGER...

Available from 15th March 2002

Available at most branches of WH Smith,
Tesco, Martins, Borders, Eason, Sainsbury's
and most good paperback bookshops.

0402/35/MB34

FREE
2 BOOKS
AND A SURPRISE GIFT!

We would like to take this opportunity to thank you for reading this Mills & Boon® book by offering you the chance to take TWO more specially selected titles from the Modern Romance™ series absolutely FREE! We're also making this offer to introduce you to the benefits of the Reader Service™—

★ FREE home delivery   ★ FREE gifts and competitions
★ FREE monthly Newsletter   ★ Exclusive Reader Service discount
★ Books available before they're in the shops

Accepting these FREE books and gift places you under no obligation to buy; you may cancel at any time, even after receiving your free shipment. Simply complete your details below and return the entire page to the address below. *You don't even need a stamp!*

YES! Please send me 2 free Modern Romance™ books and a surprise gift. I understand that unless you hear from me, I will receive 4 superb new titles every month for just £2.55 each, postage and packing free. I am under no obligation to purchase any books and may cancel my subscription at any time. The free books and gift will be mine to keep in any case.

P2ZEC

Ms/Mrs/Miss/Mr ....Initials ....
BLOCK CAPITALS PLEASE

Surname ....

Address ....

....

....Postcode ....

Send this whole page to:
UK: FREEPOST CN81, Croydon, CR9 3WZ
EIRE: PO Box 4546, Kilcock, County Kildare (stamp required)

Offer valid in UK and Eire only and not available to current Reader Service subscribers to this series. We reserve the right to refuse an application and applicants must be aged 18 years or over. Only one application per household. Terms and prices subject to change without notice. Offer expires 30th June 2002. As a result of this application, you may receive offers from other carefully selected companies. If you would prefer not to share in this opportunity please write to The Data Manager at the address above.

Mills & Boon® is a registered trademark owned by Harlequin Mills & Boon Limited.
Modern Romance™ is being used as a trademark.